James Gairdner, Edward D. Morgan

Sailing Directions for the Circumnavigation of England

and for a voyage to the straits of Gibraltar - From a 15th century ms.

James Gairdner, Edward D. Morgan

Sailing Directions for the Circumnavigation of England
and for a voyage to the straits of Gibraltar - From a 15th century ms.

ISBN/EAN: 9783337316518

Printed in Europe, USA, Canada, Australia, Japan

Cover: Foto ©Andreas Hilbeck / pixelio.de

More available books at **www.hansebooks.com**

SAILING DIRECTIONS

FOR THE

CIRCUMNAVIGATION OF ENGLAND.

AND FOR A VOYAGE TO

THE STRAITS OF GIBRALTAR.

(FROM A 15TH CENTURY MS.)

EDITED, WITH AN ACCOUNT OF THE MS.,

By JAMES GAIRDNER,

OF THE PUBLIC RECORD OFFICE;

And a Glossary

By E. DELMAR MORGAN,

HON. SEC. HAKLUYT SOCIETY.

LONDON:

PRINTED FOR THE HAKLUYT SOCIETY,

4, LINCOLN'S INN FIELDS, W.C.

M.DCCC.LXXXIX.

CONTENTS.

CIRCUMNAVIGATION OF ENGLAND.

ACCOUNT OF THE MS.

AMONG the Lansdowne MSS. in the British Museum is a folio volume, No. 285 of that collection, "the greatest part of which", as we are informed in the catalogue, "formerly belonged to Sir John Paston, Knight, in the reign of Edward IV, and was copied for him by one William Ebesham, a scribe by profession". It consists of a number of short tracts, mostly relating to pageants, coronations, challenges, tournaments, and feats of arms. Chivalry was the great study and amusement of the age, and Sir John Paston shared in the general feeling. There are, however, two treatises of more considerable length ; the one a translation of Vegetius' *De Re Militari*, the other Lydgate's poetical translation of Aristotle's *De Regimine Principum*. There is also the tract here printed for the first time, containing directions for the circumnavigation of England.

That the MS., or the greatest part of it, did, as the catalogue says, formerly belong to Sir John Paston, appears at first sight to rest on indisputable evidence. There can be no doubt about the antiquity of the handwriting, and that the greater part of the

CIRCUMNAVIGATION OF ENGLAND.

ACCOUNT OF THE MS.

———

AMONG the Lansdowne MSS. in the British Museum is a folio volume, No. 285 of that collection, "the greatest part of which", as we are informed in the catalogue, "formerly belonged to Sir John Paston, Knight, in the reign of Edward IV, and was copied for him by one William Ebesham, a scribe by profession". It consists of a number of short tracts, mostly relating to pageants, coronations, challenges, tournaments, and feats of arms. Chivalry was the great study and amusement of the age, and Sir John Paston shared in the general feeling. There are, however, two treatises of more considerable length ; the one a translation of Vegetius' *De Re Militari*, the other Lydgate's poetical translation of Aristotle's *De Regimine Principum*. There is also the tract here printed for the first time, containing directions for the circumnavigation of England.

That the MS., or the greatest part of it, did, as the catalogue says, formerly belong to Sir John Paston, appears at first sight to rest on indisputable evidence. There can be no doubt about the antiquity of the handwriting, and that the greater part of the

B 2

contents was written by William Ebesham, Sir John
Paston's transcriber, of whose signature Sir John
Fenn has given us a facsimile from one of the lost
Paston letters.[1] Moreover, we have in that correspondence William Ebesham's bill, delivered to Sir
John Paston, for transcribing a MS. of precisely
similar character ; and, further, we have the description of just such a MS. in a catalogue of Sir John
Paston's books. What stronger evidence could reasonably be expected ? Taking even the last point
alone, how very exact is the following description in
an inventory of books written either by Sir John
Paston or by his brother after his death :—

"Memorandum, my boke off knyghthod and the man[er]
off makyng off knights, off justs, off Tor[neaments,] ffyght-
yng in lystys, paces holden by so[ldiers,] and chalenges,
statuts off Weer, and *De Regim[ine Principum.]*
    Valet,   . . ."[2]

Nothing could well tally more closely than this with
the contents of the Lansdowne volume. And, as if
to close the door to any other surmise, the catalogue
states that three of the smaller articles in this volume
are in Sir John Paston's handwriting, whose signature is attached to one of them at folio 42.

Nevertheless, the case is not quite so complete as
this seemingly invincible evidence would make it.
In the first place, the statement about Sir John
Paston's hand and signature is wrong. The name of
Sir John Paston does indeed occur at the end of one

[1] Fenn's *Original Letters*, vol. ii, plate v, No. 20.
[2] *Paston Letters* (new edition), iii, 301.

article, but it is certainly not a signature, nor is there any handwriting in the volume which bears the least resemblance either to that of the Sir John Paston who died in Edward IV's time, or to that of his brother John, who was knighted after him, in the days of Henry VII. This the compiler of the catalogue would probably have discovered if he had been able to examine any of the original Paston letters for comparison. But in those days they were not accessible, and his surmise, though natural, turns out to be unfounded. All that can be said is that an article written in a different hand from Ebesham's is subscribed with the words, "Quod Sir Jhon Paston", whatever that subscription may imply.

Then, as regards the notices supposed to refer to this volume in the Paston Letters. There is no doubt whatever that several of the treatises contained in this volume were actually transcribed for the first Sir John Paston by the hand of William Ebesham; for, among the documents printed by Fenn, is Ebesham's own bill for transcribing these treatises among other things.[1] The items of this account are a somewhat singular mixture of law and literature;—first, "A litill booke of Pheesyk", for transcribing which the charge is twenty pence; then, some privy seals and depositions of witnesses, some on parchment and some on paper. But the entries which concern our purpose are those at the end of the document, which are as follows:

---

[1] See *Paston Letters*, vol. ii, No. 596 (new edition), or in Fenn's edition, vol. ii, Letter xxiv.

" Item, as to the Grete Booke—First, for wryt-
yng of the Coronacion, and other tretys of
Knyghthode, in that quaire which conteyneth a
xiij levis and more, ij$^{d.}$ a lef . . . . ijs.   ij$d$.

" Item for the tretys of Werre in iiij books,
which conteyneth lx levis after ij$^{d.}$ a leaff . . . xs.

" Item, for *Othea* pistill, which conteyneth
xliij leves . . . . vijs.   ij$d$.

" Item, for the Chalengs, and the Acts of
Armes, which is xxviij$^{ti.}$ lefs . . . . iiijs. viij$d$.

" Item for *De Regimine Principum*, which conteyneth xlv$^{ti.}$ leves, after a peny a leef, which is
right wele worth . . . . iijs.   ix$d$.

" Item, for Rubrissheyng of all the booke . . iijs. iiij$d$."

If "the Grete Booke" comprised all the articles
mentioned in these different items[1] it certainly bore
a wonderful resemblance to the Lansdowne volume,
and much certainly might be said in favour of their
identity ; but there are difficulties in the way.   Of
these five consecutive items four do indeed corre-
spond in character and substance with different portions of the volume, and in two of these cases the
number of leaves which the tract actually occupies is
precisely what is stated in the account.   But it is

---

[1] There can be little doubt that this is implied ; for the writer
acknowledges he had been paid some of the items in his bill, and
it is the " Grete Booke" for which he specially demands payment
in the accompanying letter. Moreover, though his arithmetic is a
little unsatisfactory, it appears that the sum remaining due to him
was 41s. 1d., of which, as we may infer from the note added to the
amount, the principal part was for the " Grete Booke".   Indeed,
his charge for this, if I do not misread, is 27 shillings (" unde pro
magno libro scripto, xxvij *(sic)*, cum diu' chal"; which last expression evidently means *cum diversis chalengiis*, not *cum diurnali
challengiorum*, as I suggested in a foot-note in the *Paston Letters*).

singular, to say the least, that the order in which they stand in the MS. is different from that of the account. Moreover, the "tretys of Werre", in four books, covers not sixty leaves, but only fifty-three, and a quarter of a page more. Also the treatise *De Regimine Principum* occupies, not forty-five leaves, but only forty-four; and, further, there is nothing in the volume corresponding to "*Othea* pistill". That expression we know denotes a treatise upon Wisdom. The Greek invocation 'Ω θεὰ had been converted by the ignorance of the Middle Ages into a proper name, and we meet with this divinity addressed in one poem :—

"Othea, of prudence named godesse."[1]

But nothing like a treatise on Wisdom filling forty-three leaves of paper can be found in the Lansdowne volume ; and, if this be altogether a separate treatise, how comes it to be thus inserted in the account among items which are distinctly portions of the "Grete Booke"? Nor do our difficulties end even here ; for, surely, in his charges for transcribing the book Ebesham might have been expected to follow the order of the contents of the book itself. But, after "the Coronacion and other tretys of knighthode" which undoubtedly stand first in the volume, he goes on to notice "the tretys of Werre", which begins at f. 83,[2] before the Challenges and Acts of Arms

---

[1] *Third Report of the Historical MSS. Commission*, p. 188.

[2] I follow the original contemporary foliation, in Roman figures, which, it is to be regretted, any one ever attempted to supersede, though it might have been supplemented by modern figures where it is discontinued.

which form the second portion of the volume beginning at f. 14.   And it must not be supposed that
the contents have been bound up in later times in a
different order from that in which they originally
stood; for the leaves are numbered in a contemporary
hand from leaf 1 to 86, and though for a few pages
this foliation (strangely enough) is dropped, it is
resumed quite correctly at folio 100, and goes on to
144 in the same original hand, after which it is con-
tinued in antique numerals, but in a more modern
hand, as far as f. 155.   If, therefore, this MS. be the
"Grete Book", referred to by Ebesham in his account,
it is certain that he cited the contents in a wrong
order, made two slips as to the number of leaves
each article occupied, and entered one charge for
a treatise not in the book at all among those which
really do belong to it.

Such an amount of error is scarcely conceivable in
a bill so methodically drawn up, even though the
writer was, as he himself says, at the time driven to
live in sanctuary to escape his creditors.   Yet, it is
not altogether impossible, Ebesham may have written
out the items only from memory and put things
down in a wrong order.   There is, however, another
theory which, I am inclined to think, will account
more satisfactorily for these discrepancies.   A pro-
fessional transcriber, no doubt, copied and recopied
the same treatises often for various customers, and
though the contents are very much the same there
is nothing positively to show that the Lansdowne
volume was Sir John Paston's copy of the "Grete

Booke" at all. On the contrary, the expression, "Quod Sir Jhon Paston", strikes me, upon reflection, as if it might fairly imply that the article to which it is appended was an extract from one of Sir John Paston's MSS., taken by his permission, and that these words were added to verify the authority.

What is known of the history of the volume seems rather to suggest that it was compiled for the use of an officer of arms. The earliest owner of it, whose name we can positively ascertain, was Sir Thomas Wriothesley, Garter, in whose handwriting, as Sir F. Madden believed, some of the later entries are written, and whose initials, "T. Wr.", may be seen on the first leaf. Now, Sir Thomas lived within a generation certainly of the first owner of all, for he died in 1534 ; and, after his day it passed through the hands of a long line of heralds, bequeathed apparently from one to another as an official heirloom. As stated in the catalogue, "it appears to have been in the possession of Sir Gilbert Dethick, and his son Sir William Dethick, Garter King-at-Arms, and afterwards became the property of Richard Saint George, Clarencieux". The notices of its further descent are here a little interrupted. Richard, or rather Sir Richard Saint George, the friend of Camden, Spelman, and Sir Robert Cotton, was the father of a line of heralds extending to the days of George I, and we may reasonably believe that it must have remained in his family at least for a generation or two. But the next person, in whose possession we find evidence that it existed, is Sir Joseph

Jekyll, Master of the Rolls in the reign of George I and II. From him, however, it again passed into the possession of a herald, the industrious antiquary Oldys, who made considerable use of it in his article on Caxton in the *Biographia Britannica*. After his death it was, doubtless, acquired by the first marquis of Lansdowne, and thus became a portion of the Lansdowne library, now in the British Museum.

So much for the history of a MS., the general contents of which possess an interest for the historian and the antiquary quite apart from that of the one brief article here edited for the Hakluyt Society. It only remains to say that that article is written in the clear business-like hand of William Ebesham, and though the punctuation is defective, and the spelling, of course, not more uniform than that of the very best penmen of the age, there is not a single letter throughout which is either illegible or uncertain, except where combinations occur of the letters *m*, *n*, *u*, and *i*. These letters, as every one knows who is at all familiar with the handwritings of the period, were invariably expressed, when in the middle of a word, merely by a number of upright strokes called *minums;* no difference whatever was made in the formation of the letters *n* and *u*, and the *i*'s had no dots to distinguish them. Hence, ambiguities may occur occasionally as to the spelling of proper names, only known to us through a unique mediæval MS. like the present.

SAILING DIRECTIONS

FOR THE

CIRCUMNAVIGATION OF ENGLAND

AND FOR

A VOYAGE TO THE STRAITS OF GIBRALTAR.

BERWIK lieth south and north of Golden stonys, the Ilonde and Berwik haven lien west north west and Est South est. And fro Vamborugh to the poynt of the Ilond the cours lieth north and South. And beware of the golde stonys it folowith North north west, and quarter tide be owte fro Tilmouth to Fenyn Ilonde the cours is North northwest and South South est. And Tilmouth is tide north est and South west betwene the hedelonde and houndeclif fote the cours is northwest and southest. And it flowith west southwest and Est northest. And at Whitevies half and fro Houndeclif fote to Humbre the cours is south est and be south, northwest and by north. Fro Leyrnes to the Hedelonde the cours is north northwest and south south est, at the Hedelonde the streme settith North West and Southest, and it flowith on the londe of Holdernes northest, and quarter tide in the faire way, and at Hedelonde quarter tide and half. And yif ye go from Leirnes to the Shelde ye shall goo Est Southest for to go cleene of Resande and by South. And yif ye have an ebbe go southest and by Est. And yif ye go fro the spone to the shelde, and that the wynde be at Northwest your cours is Southest till ye be passid Welbank. And in well it flowith est and west, And there goeth half streme undir Rothir. And at the shelde it flowith on the londe West north west and half streme undir Rothir by the londe till ye come to Winterbornes. And from Wyntirburnes till ye coome to

Cukle rode it flowith on the londe northwest and quarter tide and half quarter undir Rothir. And yif ye goo fro the shelde to the Holmes, and it be in the nyght, ye shall go but xviij fadome fro the coste till the gesse that ye be past Limber[1] and Urry, and to the estermare cours till ye come to xiiij fadome. And go your cours South southest till ye be passid the Holmes, but the moost wisedome is to abide till it be day. From Kirkleholmys to Orfordnesse and the wynde be on the londe saile your way is south and by west it flowith on the londe south southest, and at the Holmys hede quarter tide, fro Orfordnesse to Orwell waynys the cours is southwest and it flowith south southest. And in Orwell haven within the weris south and north, and yif ye go oute of Orwell waynys to the Naisse ye must go south west fro the Nasse to the merkis of the spetis your cours is west south-west, and it flowith south, and by Est bring your markis to gidre that the parissh steple be owte by est. the abbey of Seint Hosies than go your cours on the spetis south till ye come to x ffadome or xij. than go your cours with the horse shoo south southwest, and yif it be on flode come not by in viij. ffadome and that shall bryng you to a xj. or xij. fadome, than go your cours in to Temesse with the grene bank west southwest, and at the hors shoo it flowith south and north, and oute of Orwell waynys for to goo oute at the slade your cours is est southest for cause of the rigge and the Rokkis, till ye com till xv ffadome depe and for the long sande than ye may goo south southest till ye come to xvij. or xviij. fadome depe. than must ye go south a glas or two by cause of the Rokke. than goo south southwest, and seke up Tenet, and seke up vj fadome on the brakis. than go your cours south it is your fairway, and at the Knak, in the Kentisshe See it flowith south, and at the northhede of Godewyn the streme renneth to the south south west, and it flowith from Tenet unto Wiet on both sides on the maylaunde south southest, at Sand-

---

[1] The name may be read either Limber or Lunber.

wiche at Davyes gate south and in the Doownys goth half
tide under Rothir and yif ye Ride in the Doowns and will go
into Sandwiche haven Rere it by turnyng wynde at an est
south of the moone, and yif it be a flowyng wynd ye may
abide the lenger, and yif ye be bounde to Caleis haven and
Ride in the Doowns, and the wynde be west south west, ye
must Rere at a North north est moone and gete you into your
merkis. the steple into the fan, than go your cours Est southest ovir and aftir your wynde and your tide serve your cours.
And loke ye secke Caleis haven at a south southest mone or
els at a South and by est. And yif ye turne in the Downes
come not nere Godwyn than ix. fadome ne not nere the brakis
than v. fadome. Fro Seint Margret steyers and ye will go
with Dengenes, your best way is south south west and seke
you xviij. fadome depe be twene seint Margaret steyers and
Dengenesse goeth half tide, and fro Dengenes to Hildirnes
your cours is Est and West Dengenes. and the watir of Sowm
lyeth est south est and west north west, Dengenes and depe
southest and by est Northwest and by west, Dengenes and
ye have xxᵗⁱ· fadome depe. Westsouthwest and est north est
that is your cours along the see, and at Dengenes is half and
half quarter tide and south unto Hastyngis half tide as by
cheffe quarter tide Be chif and Depe south est and northwest.
Bechif and the Seyn hede south and north, the Ile of
Arundele and Strotarde south southest and north northwest
the Seyne hede and Wolneshorde¹ south est and northwest
Berfletnes and Wolneshorde south southest and north north
west The Chapell of Hoggis and the Nedles south and north.
the Hagge be est Rokesnes and Wolneshorde south and by
west north and by est Wolneshorde and Garnesey southe
southwest and quarter tide at Wolneshorde. Fro Wolneshorde unto the Ligge of Seint Elenes is half tide undir
Rothir. And from Seint Elenes to Chakkeshorde is half tide

¹ The name may be Wolveshorde, as there is no difference in fifteenth
century writing between the letters n and u, and the latter continually
stands for v.

and a south moone makith high watir within Wiet th
nedlis and the forne lieth south west, and by west north es
and by est the nedlis and Cornelande est and west. At th
nedlis it flowith south est and by south fro the nedles t
Portlonde the cours is west south west and est north est a
the Polketh in haven it flowith northwest and southest, an
in the fairway south southest and north northwest. At Way
mouth within havyn Est and West at the Bill at Portlond
south south est and north northwest, the Seyne hede at Port
londe and Garnesey south and north, Seyne hede and the ha
wode be west Dertmouth est and by south west and be nortl
Abottysbury and the forne lieth northest and south wes
Portlande and bery land is est and by north west and b
south. bery laund and the Stert west south west and E:
northest, betwene Portlande and the Stert ever (?)[1] havyn
tide est and west betwene Bery londe and the Londis ende (
Englonde there is half tide. In the fairway betwene th
Start and Lisart the cours is est and west. And beware (
the hidre stonys. All the havens be full at a west sout
west moone betwene the Start and Lisart. the Londis end
and Lisard lieth est southest and west northe west. At tl
Londis ende lieth Raynoldis stone. A litill birth of but xi
fadom shall lede you all be owten hym and south south we:
of the Landes ende lieth the gulf. the langshippis and tl
landende lien north northwest and south southest. And
flowith west southwest and half tide undre Rothir by lond
but none the long shippis and seint mary Sande of Cille lit
west south west and est northest Seint Mary of Cille an
Uschante lien northwest and by north south est and by sout
Cille and the seyne lien south southest and north northwes
the seyne and Huschaunt lieth south and north Huscham
and the pople hope lien north and by west south and be e:
Huschaunt and Lisard north and south, Lisarde and seit

---

[1] *Ever* or *euer*. The reading may be "Sterteuer" intended to be rea
as one word. though written like two.

Mary sande of Cille est and west but beware the gulf.   Saint
mary sande and the forne northwest and southest the forne
and the poplehope north northwest and south southest the
forne and lisard north and by west south and by est. the
forne and the grey be est.   Falmouth north and south. the
forne and the Ram hede south southwest and north north est,
huschaunt and the Ram hede northest and by north southwest and by south, be forne and berylonde north est and by
north south west and be south, the start and baspalis north
and south, baspalis and the Ramhede north and by este South
and by west, Garnesey and the hey wode be west Dertmouth
west north west and est southest.   In spayne and bretayne
this is the cours and the tide. fro Seint Mahuys unto baspalis
the cours is est northest and west south west, and open of
baspalis lieth the langas it flowith Est and west on the
cooste. the Langas and the estbrigge lye south and by west
northest and by Est till ye come into your fairway yif ye be
bounde Estwarde ye shall go north est, and yif ye be bounde
westwarde ye shall go west southwest till ye com ayenst the
forne.   At the forne goth half tide betwene Huschaunt and
thee forne the Cours of the Chanell of Seint Mathyus and
ye go withoute the bradreth ye must go for to go clene of all
daungers your cours is south and by est north and by west,
but wynde makith cours.   And at Seynt Matheus it flowith
Est north est and south southwest.   At the forlande of
fontenes it flowith southwest and northest, but a man that
ridith in the way of odierene at an ankre, he may begyn to
rere at an est southest moone for to turne   And the wynde
be at the north est or hou so evir it be fro the forelonde of
fontenes to the straitis of Marrok.   A south west mone
makith hiest watir by the see coste, and in the updraughtis
it dooth not so the forelonde of fontenes and penmarke lien
north west and southest And Penmark and the saine north
west and be west south est and be est the saine and by
Huschaunt north and south Penmarke   And be like west

north west and est south est, beware of Vas glenaunt the
streeme settith southwest and north est go fro the same
southest and by est, and ye bee in lx. fadome depe and :
and ye shall fall with eleron, than go your cours with the
pelehede south est and by south and ye be in xij. fadome
depe, And than shall lede you wᵗoute the poullis.   Fro the
Pelis ye must go est north est till ye be above the piper
than go est and by north for cause of the horshoo.   And
than ye may go from opyn on the blake shore est southes
till ye come as high in geronde as talamont, for the grounde:
on the southir side lyen ferr oute, and arne shore too, for y
may come no nere them than vij. fadome.   And when y
come anens talamont ye shall go with Castillion south south
est And beware of the mydill grounde use and be lile lier
south est and northwest be like and the pekelerre ly
west northwest and est south est the tutport and the peli
lyen west northwest and est southest the pelis and the
borugh of baion south and north. go fro the pelis of Amian
west southwest,   And go clene of all the coste of Spayne and
ye shall come by Siete of Cap' finestre all high up use and
macheschaco southest and by south northwest and be north
belile and seint Tony south and north. belille and sein
Andrews north and by est south And by west belille and
Ortingere southwest and by south north est and by north
Belille and the Cap' fenister southwest and by west north
est and by est the saine and the bokowe of Vaion south es
and northwest Maschechaco and Sayne southest and by south
northwest and be north the sayne and seint Tony south
south est and north northwest, Seint Andrews And the Seyn
north and by west south and by Est Seint Sebastians and
the saine south and north.   Ortinger and Huschaunt soot
south west and north northest the forelonde of fontenes and
the cap' Fenistre northest and south west be ware of the
saine fro the bokowe of bayon to the cap fenistre the fai
way is est and west, the cap fenistre and the berlinge soot

and north the birlingis and the Rokkes seynter south south
est and north northwest cape seint Vincent and cape seint
marie est and by south west and by north cape seint Marie
and Caleis maly southest and by est north west and by west
Calus and the River of civell south est and by south north
west and by north, Cape seint marie and the straitis south
est and northwest the straites est north est and west southwest, Cape fenister and mews nesse north and by west south
and by est Cape fenister and clere in Irlonde north and
South cape fenistre and cille north north est and south south
west clere and the bokowe of baion southest and northwest
clere and seint Tony in Spayne north north west and southe
southest clere and Ortingere north and by west south and by
est clere and the saine est southest and west northwest
clere and cille south est and northwest, cille and the holde
hede of Hinderfforde south yest and by est north west and by
west A newe cours and tide betwene Englonde and Irlonde
the Londis end and the holde hede of Hinderforde west north
west and est southest shipmanhede of cille and the seven
stonys southest and northest, the long shippis and the vij.
stonys est and west the Londis ende and the Yokelis north
west and southest the Londis ende and the toure of Watirforde north northwest and south south est, the toure of
Watirforde and the toure of Velafade north and south, the
Londis ende and saltais north and by west south and by est
Tuskarde and long shippis north and south freston herde and
smal of skidwale north and by est south and by west Ferston-
horde and seint Thomas forlande on the west side of Milforde
north north est and soth south west, est and west it flowith
within the havyn and half streme vndir Rothir and w^{t}oute
it renneth north est and southwest, shipmanhede and
mylford north est and by north south west and by south.
Shipmanhede and Londay north est and southwest. And be
ware of the vij. stonys Frestonhorde and Londay north est
and by north south west and by south. Londay and Calday

U

north and south. fro the Londis ende to Londay it flowith west southwest and est northest fro Londay to the Holmys est and by north west and by south be ware of Iron groundis and of your stremes of flode for they sitten north est on the Iron groundis. And on ebbe spare not to goo for the streemys of Briggewatir sit west norwest. And beware of Columsonde it flowith fro Londay to the Holmys est and west and fro the Holmys for to go clene of the Wasshe groundis and of Longbors the cours is north. And ye come on ebbe and sith go est and north est with Portis hede but yif ye have a quarter tide at the flat holme ye may goo est north est or est and by south and go ovir Langborde with Ketils wode with a gode ship, for ye shall have iij. fadome on the sonde or more by that ye come there betwene the holmys and Ketilsworde and Portishede it flowith west, and by north est and by south at Kyngrode it flowith est and west. And set on no lesse watir above the holmys than xij. fadome at the leest, Seint Thomas forlonde and stalmay lieth north-west and southest. All that see betwene Irlonde and Walis goth half tide under Rothir, londay and the old hede of Hindilforde lye west and by north and est and by south. And yif ye be bounde[1]
go west northwest. And ye shall go clene of Kidwall and small and ye have any ebbe the streme settith north north est and south southwest. And there is half tide undir Rothir for it flowith on loude est and west, fro tuscarde to the olde hede of Hindilforde to Clere in Irlonde the cours is west and by south est and by north, Clere and mews nesse and thursay north west and southest, thursay and the lewe north northwest and south southest, the sowde of blaskay lye north and south, blaskay and the Ackiles north and south. Blaskay and the stakis of Connothe north north-est and South southwest, but thou must go north and by est for a Rokke the stakis of Romney. And the Londes end of

---

[1] Here half a line is left blank in the original MS.

Irlonde north northest and south southwest.   And so thou must go to the Ilonde of Torre the stakis of Conney and southwest and northest.   And fro the stakes of Conney to the legge of Rabyn the cours is west southwest and est north est, the sonde and the forelonde be est Loswill lieth west southwest and est north est, but be ware of the Rokke in the Bay of Loswill.   Fro the forlonde of Loswill to Donsmares hede the cours is west north west and est southest, the sounde of Ranseynes the same cours with Benoster fro Tuscarde to Donsmere hede it flowith by the see cost west south west and est north est, But in the updraughtis it dooth not soo, fro tuscarde to the redebank it is half tide undir Rothir. Fro saltais to tuscarde the cours is est and west, fro the tuscarde to the hede of the skarres for to go clene of all the gronde betwene tuscarde and Dalcay the cours is north est and south southwest, fro the Skarris unto Arglas the cours is north and south,   Fro Arglas ye shall go with Capman eylond south southest and north northwest but and ye be bounde to Capman ylonde ye shall go north and by west, for cause of ij Rokkes that lien in the wey.   And yif ye be bounde south warde ye shall go south est and by south.   Fro Capman ylonde to the forlonde of Welnerferth ye shall goo north northest and south southwest, fro the forlonde of Wolnderfrith to benestore south southest and north north-west it flowith on the coste betwene tuscarde and beneford, south southest and north northwest, betwene Capman Ilonde and Donblak.   And by south Arglas there goth quarter tide undir Rothir Capman ylonde and the Ile of Man the south-ende lieth south and by est northwest.   And by west the Ilonde of Man and Arglas Est north est and west south west, the Ile of Man and Lambey Ilonde north est and south west, the Holbe and the Holy hede est and west Lambay and tha Ramsair north and south, the chirch of Wiklowe and the Ransires south southest. but a man that ridith in the Rode of Wiklowe must go oute of the chirch of Wiklowe south est and northwest, Tuscarde and the Ransere est and west, the toure of Watirford and gresholme west and be north est and be south. All that see goth half tide betwene the smale and Skidwhalles and the bersays. And it flowith est and west on the mayne londe and at at[1] the Ramseir north and south the stremys renne in the sonde and be owten the Bisshoppis and his clerkis north northwest and south south est, sculke holme and the sonde of Ramseirs north and south And beware the Rok men callith Sampson for he lieth at the south point at seint Davy side. And kepe more nere the Ilonde than the mayne londe till ye be passid the point and thorowe the sande, than go north till ye come at a nothir Rok. And for cause of that Rok ye must go north and by west or els north and by est for north is even with the Rok. And the name of the Rok is called the Kep', and he lieth undir the watir but it brekith upon hym And the breche shewith, And than your cours is north northest for to go with barseis stremys, and seint Davies londe northest and southwest. And so go your cours north northest and south south west till ye come to Ire north west upon Scotlande the Holy Hede and the Ile of man north and by est south and be west. And yif ye go to Chestir ye shall go fro the scarris till ye come anens the Castell of Rotlonde your cours is west southwest and est northest. And take your saught on the mayne londe of Wales Rotlonde and the Redebank in Chestre watir north and South.[2]

Opyn oo grounde there is wose and sonde togidir and it is bein xij. or xiiij. fadome or xvj. fadome depe. Upon opertus Mamoschaunt there is stynkyng wose and xij fadome depe. opon opertus antiage there is blake sande opon o the taile of ars is xxiiij[ti.] or xxvj. fadome depe there is grete grey sonde and smale blake stonys and grete whit shellis among upon of use there is l. or lx. fadome depe wosy sonde. Open

---

[1] *Sic.* "at" repeated.

[2] Here a small space is left blank in the MS.

one Liere there is stremy grounde and white shellis. upon o
belille there is in lx. fadome or lxx. smale diale sonde
Opyn of Penmarke there is in l. fadome blak wose Opyn
the same in lx. fadome there is sandy wose and blak fischey
stonys among Opyn of Huschaunt in l. or lx. fadome there is
redd sande and blak stonys and white shellis among betwene
Cille and Huschaut there is grete stremy grounde with
white shellis among withoute Cille west south west of hym
the grounde is Rede sonde and white shellis amonge, between Cille and Lesarde the grounde is white sonde and
white shellis shellis[1] Among Opyn Lesarde is grete stone as it
were benys and it is raggid stoon Opyn of Dudman in xl
fadome there is rede sande and whit shellis and small blak
stonys amonge Opon oporte londe there is feir white sande
and xxiiij^ti. fadome with Rede shellis therein, And in xiiij.
or xvj. fadome there is rokky grounde and in sumplace there
is feir cley grounde Opon a Wiet there is fere hard platmer
grounde. And the faire way in xxx^ti. fadome there is white
chalky grounde Opyn o bechefe there is sande and gravell to
gidir in xx^ti. fadome depe. Here be the groundis of Inglonde
bretayne and Cille. And ye come oute of Spayne. And ye
bee at capfenister go your cours north northest. And ye
gesse you ij. parties ovir the see and be bounde into sebarne
ye must north and by est till ye come into Sowdyng, And
yif ye have an C. fadome depe or els iiij.x̄. than ye shall go
north in till the sonde ayen in lxxij. fadome in feir grey
sonde And that is the Rigge that lieth betwene clere and
Cille than go north till ye come into sowdyng of woyse. and
than go your cours est north est or els est and by north and
ye shall not faile much of Stepilhorde he risith all rounde as
it were a Coppid hille. And yif ye be three parties ovir the
see and ye be bounde into the narowe see and ye go north
northest and by north till ye come into sowdyng of an hun-

---

[1] So in MS., repeated.

drith fadom depe than go your cours north est till ye come
into iiij fadome depe.   And yif it be stremy grounde it is
betwene Huschaunt and cille in the entry in the Chanell of
Flaundres.   And so go your cours till ye have lx. fadome
depe. than go est northest along the see, etc.

INTRODUCTORY REMARKS TO GLOSSARY.

" Gentyll maryners on a bonne vyage,
Hoyce vp the saylo, and let God stere
In ye bonauenture making your passage.
It is ful see the wether fayre and clere,
The nope tydes shall you nothing dere,
A see hord mates S. George to borow,
Mary and John, ye shal not nede to fere,
But with this boke to go safe thorow."

(The Rutter of the Sea—Prologue.)

THE curious treatise printed in the foregoing pages came into the possession of the Hakluyt Society in 1880, through Mr. Gairdner, of the Public Record Office, who had it transcribed for the Camden Society. Finding its interest, however, to be purely geographical, and therefore more suitable for a Society like ours, he transferred it, together with his prefatory remarks, to my predecessor, Mr. Clements Markham. The printed sheets have been lying by ever since, waiting an opportunity of incorporating them with some other kindred work. Such an opportunity has at last been afforded by the issue of the present volume. But in order to make these old sailing directions intelligible to our readers it was obvious that some kind of a commentary was necessary. This I have attempted in the accompanying glossary, and have added a map on which the names of places are marked in their old and modern form.

In identifying the names of places, the following works have been consulted : *The Lighting Colomne, or Sea Mirrour*, by Peter Goos, printed at Amsterdam in 1658 ; *The English Coasting Pilot, or Sea Mirrour*, by Casparus Lootsman (*i.e.*, Caspar the Pilot), also published at Amsterdam in 1693 ; Seller's *Coasting and English Pilots* (1670-1680); Grenville Collins' *Coasting Pilot*, 1693 ; *A Description and Platte of the Seacoast*, author unknown, printed in 1653 ; Ortelius' *Atlas*, 1570 ; Saxton's *Atlas*, 1579 ; Imray's *Sailing Directions*, Norie's *Sailing Directions*, revised by

Hobbs ; Burat's *Côtes de France ;* Camden's *Britannia ;* and the *English and French Admiralty Charts.*

Many of the names appeared, at first sight, hopelessly difficult, and it was only after patient investigation and research that their meaning became clear—for who would suspect that " Leyrnes" referred to the well-known town of Wainfleet, or that " the Shelde" was no other than the now fashionable sea-bathing place of Cromer; that " Whitvies", " the Spone", and " Wolveshorde" were respectively Whitby, the Spurnhead, and Dunnose Point ? Passing to the other side of the English Channel, or the Channel of Flanders, as it was then called, we find such names as " the Hagge" for Cape La Hague, " Hoggis" for Cape La Hougue, " Berfletnes" for Cape Barfleur, and many other curiosities. Turning to obsolete terms, " Undir Rothir" occurs several times, and always with reference to tides. We have, " At the Shelde (*i.e.,* Cromer), it floweth on the londe westnorthwest and half streme (stream) *undir Rothir* by the londe till ye come to Winterbornes (*i.e.,* Winterton ness)"; and again, " from Wyntirburnes till ye coome to Cukle rode (Kirkley road) it flowith on the londe northwest and quarter tide and half quarter *undir Rothir.*" So, again, in the Downs we are told it goeth " half tide *undir Rothir*".

This expression " under Rothir" presented considerable difficulty. The Dictionaries threw no light upon it, but rather led me off the scent by giving "Rothir", an old form of "rudder"; and many were my attempts to account for the tide running differently under the rudder from what it did under any other part of the ship.

At the British Museum Library, however, I came upon a little book entitled *The Rutter of the see with the hauens rodes, soundynges, kennynges, wyndes, flodes and ebbes, daungers and coastes of dyuers regions, with the lawes of the yle Auleron and the iudgementes of the see, with a Rutter of the Northe added to the same.* The first part of this work is a translation by Robert Copland, a pupil of the famous Caxton, of a French *routier* (Angl. rutter). The last part, compiled by Richard Prowde in 1541, is a reproduction of our " Sailing Directions", breaking off at Dartmouth. No clue is given as to the true authorship of the treatise by the compiler, who merely associates his own name with it. I am inclined, however, to attribute its origin to Clement Paston of Oxnead, Norfolk, a great navigator in the time of Henry VIII. He was fourth son of Sir William Paston, and distinguished himself in the wars of that period.

On comparing this printed version with our transcript I find the words " Undir Rothir" rendered "under other"; and in William Bourne's *Regiment of the Sea,* a sixteenth century treatise on navigation, directions as to tides are also followed by the words "under the other". Thus we are told (leaf 14, back), that " from Fairely to Be(a)chy (Head) it runneth quarter tide *under other*"; and on leaf 15, "It floweth all alongst the coast of Flanders from the Wildings to Calys (Calais), a south and by East moone ; and so runneth halfe tide *under the other."*

The meaning of " under Rothir" now becomes clear, for the late Sir George Airy, in his treatise on " Tides and Waves" in the *Encyclopædia Metropolitana,* says that the tides in the English Channel claim notice as having been the subject of careful examination by many persons, English and French. It appears that in the upper part of the Channel the water flows up the Channel nearly three hours after high water and runs down nearly three hours after low water. This continuance of the current after high water, if it last three hours, is called by sailors " tide and half tide"; if it last one hour and a half, it is called " tide and quarter tide". It is obvious that the tidal currents are then flowing in opposite directions, one under the other, and thus we have a satisfactory explanation of the term " under Rothir", without following up the intricate subject of tides any further. (Cf. *Manual of Tides and Tidal Currents,* by the Rev. S. Haughton.)

The identification of Cromer with " the Shelde" of our MS. was another difficulty, for although the names occur together in two old " Sailing Directions" translated from the Dutch, in one marked on a map as "Dager and *Schild*" on the coast, a little to the north-west of Cromer, in the other it occurs in the text as follows: " From the poynt of Cromer or *Schield* to the Tessel (*i.e.,* Texel) the course is East"—yet in none of the English charts, maps, or coasting pilots does the name Shelde or Shild appear near or with reference to Cromer, nor from inquiries made on the spot could I learn of any such name having been connected with the place. Possibly "Dager and Shild" may have something to do with the "Dogger bank", and Dutch navigators in those times may have shaped their course from a point a little above Cromer in order to pass safely between that dangerous shoal and Well Bank to the south of it in crossing to Holland.   However this may be, the fact remains proved that "the Shelde" of our MS. is identical with Cromer, a place of some maritime importance up to the middle of the 16th century. (Cf. *History of Norfolk*, by W. B. Rye, p. 250.)

With regard to another identification, "Ile of Arundele", I have endeavoured to show how Arundel might have been in early times an island.   On referring, however, to Richard Prowde's version, I find that he has "Hiland (High land) of Arundel" in the same passage.   This of course throws quite a different light on the words.   It may easily be imagined that, through ignorance or carelessness of the transcriber, "Hiland" may have become changed into "Iland", and this again into "Ile".   I have, however, allowed my glossary note to stand, so that the reader may decide the point for himself.

In conclusion, I beg to acknowledge, with thanks, kind advice and suggestions received from Dr. Richard Garnett of the British Museum, and from Admiral Brine.

E. DELMAR MORGAN.

GLOSSARY.

Abbotysbury—Abbotsbury, on the coast of Dorsetshire.

Ackiles, The—Achil Head, on Achill Island, off the coast of Mayo.

Anens—Against, opposite.

Antiage, pertus—Pertuis d'Antioche, the passage between Ile de Ré and Ile d'Oleron, leading to Rochelle. The passage takes its name from some rocky banks called the "Antioches".

Arglas—Ardglass, east coast of Ireland, a few miles above St. John's Point.

Ars, Taile of—Pointe d'Arseaux, now called St. Martin's Bank, extending eastward from Ile de Ré to the middle of the channel leading to Rochelle. Ars steeple was one of the marks for the navigation of these waters.

Arundele, Ile of—Old charts represent Arundel on a peninsula, with its promontory stretching far out seaward, and the wide estuaries of two rivers, the Arun and Adur, on either side. This probably explains the term "Isle of Arundel". "We must bear in mind", says a writer in the *Sussex Archæological Collections* (vol. xi, 93), "that the whole of the levels of the river Arun were covered by water every tide, and not confined to a narrow channel as now, and that to facilitate a passage through this valley without interruption at all times a causeway was thrown up its whole width. . . ." Arundel itself, the *ad Decimum Lapidem* of the Romans, was originally a British town, with the river on one side, a marshy and wooded ravine on the other, and a *fosse* and *vallum* traversing the neck of land between the two. Arundel, now some distance inland, was a seaport, and is spoken of as "eminent for building ships", the forests in the vicinity supplying the material. (*but see* Introductory Remarks.)

Ayen—Again.

Baion and **Vaion**—Bayonne, at the confluence of the rivers Adour and Nieve, in lat. 43° 29′ 15″ N., and long. 1° 28′ 17″ W. from Greenwich. It contains 70,000 inhabitants, and is the chief town in the department of the Lower Pyrenees.

Baspalis (Ile de Bas)—An island off the north coast of Brittany ; the tide here rises and falls nearly thirty feet, covering half the island at flood. Hence its name of "Low Island".

Be like and **Be lile**—The island of Belle Ile, between 9 and 10 miles long and 3 or 4 miles broad. This island is lofty and steep, spacious and fertile, and its deeply indented coast affords shelter and anchorage to navigators. Its name therefore is appropriate.

Benoster—Probably Benmore, or Fair Head, north-east coast of Ireland.

Benys, *i.e.,* beans—In old sailing directions we find "Great rough stones as big as beans".

Be owten—Without, in the sense of outside.

Berfletnes—Cape Barfleur.

Berlinge and **Birlingis**—The Burlings rocks, off the coast of Portugal, in lat. 39° 25′ N., long. 9° 28′ W.

Bersays and **Barseis**—Barsey, or Bardsey Island, off the coast of Carnarvon, 70 miles N.E. ¾ E. from the Small's lighthouse, and 20 leagues E. ½ N. from the Tuskar rock. A channel 1¾ mile wide separates Bardsey Island from the mainland.

Berwik—Berwick, a fortified town on the Tweed, one of the principal sea-ports in Scotland in the 12th century. In 1482 it came finally into the possession of England.

Bery land—Berry Head, on the south side of the entrance to Torbay.

Birth—Berth, "a litill birth" would, in sailors' parlance, mean a wide distance.

Bisshoppis and his Clerkis—The Bishop and his clerks, a number of dangerous rocks lying N.W. of Ramsey Island, off the coast of Wales.

Blake shore, The—Terre Negre, on the south shore of the entrance of the Gironde ; a fixed light now stands here.

Blaskay, The sowde of—Blasket Sound, west coast of Ireland.

Bokowe—From the Italian *bocca,* mouth or estuary of a river.

Borugh—*i.e.,* borough or town.

Bradreth, The—Brest Sound.

Brakis, The—The Brake sand, 4½ miles long, between the North Foreland and the Downs. This shoal is marked by three buoys, north, middle, and south Brake, known collectively as "the Brakes".

Breche—Breach, in the sense of breakers.

Bretayne—Brittany.

Briggewatir—Bridgewater, in the Bristol Channel.

Bycheffe and **Bechif**—Beachy Head, the remarkable headland with its high chalk cliff, 9½ leagues W. ¼ N. from Dungeness.

By in—Within.

Calday—Caldy Island, north of the entrance to the Bristol Channel.

Caleis Maly and **Calus**—Cadiz.

Cap' finistre and **fenister**—Cape Finisterre.

Capman eylond—Copeland or Copland Island, 2 miles N.E. ½ N. from Donaghadee, east coast of Ireland.

Castillion—On the south or Médoc shore of the Garonne, the modern Castelnau.

Chakkeshorde—Probably Chichester (also called in old sailing directions Chaikeshord) ; the termination "horde" is merely the German "ord", modern German "ort", a place.

Chestir—Chester.

Cille—The Scilly Isles.

Civell, River of—River of Seville, or Guadalquivir.

Clene—Clean, *i.e.,* clear.

Clere—Cape Clear, the southernmost point of Ireland.

Columsonde—The Culver sand, a dangerous and extensive flat to the north-ward of Bridgewater ; a narrow ridge of this sand dries for the extent of 3 miles, with long spits at each end.

Connothe and **Conney, The Stakis of**—The Stags of Connaught, some rocks off Broadhaven Bay, county Mayo, west coast of Ireland.

Coppid—Topped, in the sense of overhanging masses of rock, from " Cope", whence our word "coping", e.g., coping brick.

Cornelande—Cornwall, the horn-shaped land ; the ancient name for this county being *Kernou* or *Kerniw*, the Horn, from its projecting promon-tories.

Coste—Coast.

Cukle rode—Cockle Gat, the passage forming the entrance into Yarmouth Roads, and now called Nelson's Gat. A light vessel is moored here.

Dalcay—Dalkey Island, south of Kingstown, east coast of Ireland.

Dengenes—Dungeness, also written in old sailing directions " Dongie Nesse."

Depe—Dieppe.

Dertmouth—Dartmouth.

Dial sonde—Fine sand, suitable for hour-glasses.

Doownys, The—The Downs.

Donblak—Dundalk Bay, county Louth, east coast of Ireland.

Donsmares hede and **Donsmere hede**—Dunmore Head, north coast of Ireland.

Dudman—Deadman Head, east of Veryon Bay, Cornwall.

Eleron, The—Ile d'Oleron, off the coast of the Charente, opposite the entrance to Rochefort. Oleron was also known for its laws, a body of rules for the guidance of maritime cases. These were translated into English and published about 1540. (*See* Introductory Remarks.)

Estermare cours(e)—*i.e.*, the course for sailing to the North Sea and coast of Holland.

Ever and **euer**—For "every".

Fan—Probably for vane or weathercock.

Feir and **Fere**—For " fair".

Fenyn Ilonde—Ferne or Farne Island, the largest of a group of rocky islets E. by S. 2 miles from Bambrough Castle.

Flaunders, Chanell of—The English Channel.

Flode, On—Floodtide.

Fontenes, Forlande of—Point, or Bec, du Raz, on the coast of Brittany. On its highest part stands a lighthouse, which may be seen in fine weather at a distance of six leagues. The Abbey of Fontenay is mentioned in Exchequer Rolls of the 14th century.

Forne, The—The Four, or Oven, a remarkable black rock never covered, about a mile from the north-west point of Brittany, and ten miles from Ushant lighthouse. The Passage du Four, between Ushant and the mainland, takes its name from the rock.

Garnesey—The Island of Guernsey.

Geronde—The Gironde, or Garonne, the river of Bordeaux. Many towns and villages are situated on its banks, such as Pauillac, Blaye. But its navigation is so dangerous that vessels are advised not to enter it by night and in thick weather.

Gesse, Till the (ʒe), *i.e.*, till ye guess.

Glas or two, A—Evidently referring to the hour-glass, an important accessory in navigation up to a recent period. Clocks and watches were in use in the 15th century, or earlier on shore, but it is uncertain when they were first used at sea.

Godewyn—Goodwin.

Gold stonys—Gold Stone, a dangerous rock, rather more than a mile E.S.E. from Holy Island Castle. It is very small, and visible at low water. In old sailing directions "the Plough", another sunken rock near it, was generally included in the term "Gold stones".

Grene bank—Probably the Isle of Grain, at the mouth of the Medway.

Grey, The—Probably St. Michael's Mount. The Cornish name for this isolated rock in Mount's Bay, was *Caraclowse* or *Carey Cowse*, the Gray or Hoary Rock; and Camden says the inhabitants called it so.

Gresholme—Gresholm or Grassholm Island, south of St. David's Head, South Wales, and usually the first land seen on coming towards Milford Haven from the westward.

Gulf, The—A rock S.S.W. from the Land's End, and 5 leagues E. from Scilly, marked in modern charts as "the Wolf".

Hagge, The—Cape La Hague, the headland of Normandy, opposite the Island of Alderney. It forms the north-west extremity of the peninsula of Cotentin, in the department of La Manche.

Hastyngis—Hastings.

Hay wode—Hyant wood, one of the marks for sailing into Stoke's Bay. Havant, on the coast of Hampshire, possibly takes its name from it.

Hedelonde, The—Flamborough Head, the well-known promontory on the Yorkshire coast.

Hidre stonys—Hidden stones, in the sense of sunk rocks; possibly our word "eddy" is derived from this old form of "hidden".

Hildirnes—Probably Cape Grisnez, on the French coast, formerly known as Whiteness and Blackness.

Hinderfforde, Holde hede of—The old Head of Kinsale, south coast of Ireland.

Hoggis, Chapell of—Cape La Hogue or La Hougue, on the coast of Normandy, with Capelle Road a little to the south of it. Here, in 1692, the French fleet was defeated and almost destroyed by the combined English and Dutch fleets.

Holbe, The—Probably Bantry Bay.

Holdernes—Holderness, the low-lying south-east corner of the East Riding of Yorkshire, terminated at the extreme point by Spurn Head.

Holmes, The—The Holms, a large sandy flat at the entrance into Yarmouth Roads.

Holmys, The—The Holms, two small islands lying some distance apart, but nearly in the middle of the Bristol Channel. The southernmost of the two is called Steep Holm; the other, about 2 miles from it N. by E. ½ E., is Flat Holm.

Holmys hede—The head of Holm Sand, off Lowestoft.

Holy hede—Holyhead.

Horseshoo, The—The Horse-bank and Horse-shoe Hole, an anchoring ground between the Nore and North Foreland.

Horshoo, The—Probably a bank of sand at the mouth of the Gironde. The two banks which front the river are now called *La Mauvaise* and *La Cuivre*.

Houndeclif fote—Huntley Foot, marked Huntcliff Foot on seventeenth century charts.

Hushaunt. (*See* **Uschante.**)

Ilonde, The—Holy Island, or Lindisfarne, about 1½ mile from the mainland. The course and distance from Bambrough Castle to the south point of Holy Island are N. ¾ W., 4¼ miles.

Ire—Point of Air, S.E. by E. ¾ E., distant 19 miles from Great Orme's Head, at the entrance to the river Dee; or, more probably, Point of Ayr, the northernmost point of the Isle of Man.

Iron groundis—Probably referring to the iron-bound rocky coast south of the Bristol Channel, extending for 24 miles eastward from Ilfracombe.

It flows tide and half-tide—According to the *Seaman's Grammar*, this means that it will be high water sooner by three hours at the shore than in the offing. (*See* Introductory Remarks.)

Kep', The—Probably a rock, "the Keep"; according to our text, its position would be due north from St. David's Head.

Kidwall. (*See* **Skidwale.**)

Knak, in the Kentisshe Sea, The—The Kentish Knock, a dangerous and extensive shoal, about 19 miles N.E. ½ E. from the North Foreland lighthouse. Its length is about 7 miles, and its broadest part 2 miles.

Kirkleholmys—Kirkley Holms, off Lowestoff.

Kyngrode—King Road, between Portishead and Bristol.

Lambey Ilonde—Lambay Island, county Meath, off the east coast of Ireland, 7 miles from Howth Head. The name is probably from lamb, the animal.

Langas, The—Probably the Tour de la Lande, a leading mark for entering the Morlaix river from Ile de Bas.

Lang shippis and **Long shippis**—The Long ships, a group of rocks lying about 3 miles N.N.W. ½ W. from the south-east point of Land's End; a lighthouse now stands on the highest of them.

Lewe, The—Loop Head, west coast of Ireland, north of the Shannon.

Leyrnes and **Leirnes**—Winfleet or Wainfleet, on the coast of Lincolnshire. In seventeenth century sailing directions this place is referred to as Legerness and Lagerness.

Liere—Leyre, river and bay in Côte de Landes.

Ligge—A low-lying spit of land.

Limber and **Urry**—The Leman and Ower, two dangerous shoals lying off the coast between Foulness and Flamborough Head. These shoals are buoyed, and a light vessel is moored between them.

Lisart and **Lisard**—Lizard Point, the southmost part of England, a bold-looking land, seen in clear weather 20 miles off.

Londay—Lundy Island, off the entrance to the Bristol Channel.

Londes end of Irlande—Ireland's north point, near Malin Head.

Londis ende—Land's End, the westmost part of England.

Longbors and **Langborde**—Probably a shoal in the Bristol Channel.

Long Sande—A shoal 15½ miles long, off the mouth of the Thames.

Loswill—Lough Swilly, north coast of Ireland.

Macheschaco—Cape Machichaco, on the north coast of Spain, now marked by a lighthouse.

Mamoschaunt, Pertus—Pertuis Maumusson, the south passage between Ile d'Oleron and the Charente ; a dangerous channel, little known except to the natives.

Marrok, Straitis of—The Straits of Gibraltar.

Maylaunde—Mainland.

Merkis—Marks, *i.e.*, leading marks used in navigation.

Mews nesse—Mizan Head, south-west coast of Ireland.

Milforde and **Mylford**—Milford haven.

Mydill—Middle.

Naisse and **Nasse**—The Naze or headland of Essex, south of Harwich.

Nedles—The Needles rocks and point at the west end of the Isle of Wight.

Ne nere—Nor nearer. Cf. the use of *ne* for *nor* in "The Childe of Bristow", an early poem, published in the *Camden Miscellany*, vol. iv.

Odierne, The way of—Audierne or Hodierne Bay, is a slight indentation of the coast between Fontenay, Raz de Sein, and Penmark Point. The harbour of Audierne is tidal, and can only be entered at high water.

Open of, opyn on, and **opyn ou**—On, upon.

Opertus—The letter *o* stands for the preposition "on", the remainder of the word, sometimes spelt "porthus", is an Anglicised form of the French *pertuis*, a narrow passage between an island and the mainland, as in Pertuis d'Antioche, Pertuis Maumusson. The word is derived from the Latin *pertusus*, participle of *pertundere*, to pierce, from *per* and *tundere*, and is distinct from the Lat. *portus*, whence our "port" and the Celtic "porth".

Oporte lande—*O*, the first letter, is the preposition "on", the remainder being Portland in Dorset.

Ortingere—Cape Ortegal, in lat. 43° 46′ 30″ and long. 7° 48′ 15″ W. from Greenwich. A watch-tower is built on the summit of the cape, affording a good mark to vessels making the land.

Orwell haven—The harbour of Harwich, formed by the junction of the Stour and the Orwell.

Orwell waynys—Orwell wains or wands, at the entrance to Harwich.

Pekelerre—Picquelier Island, off the promontory of Armentier, in Poictou.

Pele hede, The—The Pole head, at the entrance of the Gironde, or river of Bordeaux. A lighthouse built on a rock called the tower of Cordouan, stands nearly midway of the entrance, and has long been esteemed the most elegant structure of the kind in Europe.

Pelis and **Pelis of Amians**—Ile du Pilier, a small island off Point de l'Herbaudière, the northwesternmost point of Noirmoutier Island.

Penmarke—Pointe de Penmarch, or Penmark Point, with two groups of dangerous rocks lying off it, known respectively as "Wester Penmarcks" and "Easter Penmarcks", off the coast of Finisterre.

Piper, The—A sandbank in the mouth of the Garonne.

Platmer—Flat, from the French "plat".

Polketh—Polkerris Bay.

Portishede—Portishead, near the mouth of the Avon.

Portlonde, Bill at—Portland Bill, a rocky peninsula projecting from the shore of Dorsetshire, 17 miles west-south-west of St. Alban's Head, and in appearance resembling the beak of a bird, whence its name.

Pople hope—Probably Hope Nose, on the north side of Torbay. *Popple*, in the Hampshire dialect, is a pebble.

Poullis, The—Probably the rocky islands which stud the west coast of France, between Poolquain and the mouth of the Loire.

Rabyn, The legge of—Rathlin Island, north-east coast of Ireland.

Ram hede—Ramehead, the west point of Plymouth Sound.

Ramsair, The, and **Ransires**—Ramsey Island, off St. David's Head.

Ranseynes, The sounde of—Ramsey Sound, between the island of this name and St. David's Head.

Raynoldis stone—Rundle or Runnell stone, a small rock between Mount's Bay and the Land's End, a most dangerous obstacle to navigation. This rock, about 4 yards long and 2 broad, is dry at low water, and covered before half-flood. In a curious account, published in 1590, of the voyage of one Richard Ferris, a Queen's messenger, in a wherry-boat from London to Bristol, the author relates how a pirate lay in wait for him near a rock called "Raynalde stones", and how he managed to escape him by passing on the inner side of the said rock, where, he says, "we went through very pleasantly". (See *Illustrations of Early English Popular Literature*, edited by Collier, vol. ii.)

Rede bank—The Red Bank—(1) a shoal in Chester water ; (2) a shoal off the south-east coast of Ireland.

Rere it, *i.e.,* raise anchor.

Re sande—Red sand shoal off the Norfolk coast.

Rigge, The—The Ridge, a rocky ledge at the entrance to Harwich.

Rokesnes—Cape Rokeine, the westernmost part of the Island of Guernsey. Rockain Castle stood here. The bay of the same name presents, says Ansted, a bristling array of rocks stretching out seawards more than two miles, and terminating on the south with the Hanois rocks.

Rokkes Seynter, The—Capo da Roca, on the coast of Portugal, in old works called Cape of Rocksemper and Roxent. Mt. Cintra is immediately to the east of it.

Rokkis, The—Probably the Cliff-foot rocks at the entrance to Harwich harbour, or the West rocks, another group between Court and Long Sand.

Romney, The stakis of—The Stags of Aranmore, rocks off the coast of Donegal.

Rothir—An obsolete form of "rudder". "Rother-nails", with shipwrights are nails with full heads, used to fasten the rudder-irons of ships. (*See* Introductory Remarks.)

Rotlande, Castell of—Rudland or Rhydland Castle, on the Clwyn or Clwyd falling into Chester water. The old castle is now a mere shell of red sandstone. It was near Rhydlan that the Welsh, under Caradoc, were defeated by the Saxons under Offa, King of Mercia.

Saine, The—Ile de Sein, or Saint, the largest of a long cluster of islands rocks, and dangers, which lie in a W.N.W. ½ westerly direction from the Bec du Raz, and are known as the Chaussée de Sein ; the island is flat in appearance and low ; its inhabitants are chiefly fishermen. A lighthouse has lately been erected on the northern point of Ile de Sein.

Saltais—The Saltees, a group of islands and rocks off the south coast of Ireland, some above and others below water at ebb tide. A light-vessel is stationed here.

Sampson—Probably a rock south of St. David's Head.

Sandwiche—One of the Cinque Ports, and a principal harbour in this part of Kent, ranking next to Hastings in precedence. In the earliest extant sea-song descriptive of a pilgrim's voyage we find—

> " For when they have take the see,
>   At Sandwyche or at Wynchelsen,
>   At Bristow, or where that hit bee,
>   Theyr herts begyn to fayle."

(*Early English Ballads,* printed for the Percy Society.)

Saught—Meaning peace, quiet ; the expression "take your saught" would therefore mean "take your rest", the perils of the voyage being over.

Scarris, The—The island and rocks called the Skerries lie about 1¾ mile from Carmel Point, Isle of Anglesey.

Sculke holme—Skokham, a rocky island 4 miles north-west from St. Ann's Point.

Sebarne—The river Severn, or Bristol Channel.

Seint Andrews—Santander, the best harbour on the north coast of Spain eastward of Cape Ortegal.

Seint Davy Side—St. David's Head.

Seint Elenes—St. Helen's, the easternmost point of the Isle of Wight. St Helen's, though an inconsiderable place, gives it name to a spacious road in which men-of-war lie. Hassell, in his *Tour of the Isle of Wight,* says there is a large farm in the parish called the Priory, it having been a cell to an abbey of Cluniac monks in Normandy.

St. Hosies—Abbey of St. Osyth's, on the coast of Essex, not far from Colchester. According to Camden, the Abbey was so named after the virgin of royal birth, who was stabbed to death here by Danish pirates.

Seint Maluys—St. Malo, in Brittany. The town stands on a small island, which it completely covers, and is joined by a causeway with the mainland. The harbour is one of the best in this part of France.

Seint Margaret Steyers—Old stairs near St. Margaret.

Seint Marie—Cape Santa Maria, on the south coast of Portugal.

Seint Mary Sande of Cille—St. Mary, the largest of the Scilly Isles. The sound, not sand, as in text, is the best and safest passage into St. Mary's Road.

Seint Matthyus and **Seynt Matheus**—Channel of the passage du Four (*q. v.*), between Ile de Sein and Pointe St. Matthieu on the mainland, at the entrance of the Bay of Brest.

Seint Sebastians—Port San Sebastian, easily discovered by its castle of La Mota, situate on the Mount Orgullo, and its old lighthouse. These are distant from each other about a mile, and may be seen at the distance of 8 or 10 leagues. The town of St. Sebastian is the capital of the district of Guipuscoa, in the province of Biscay.

Seint Thomas forlande—St. Thomas's Head, 1¾ mile from Weston Head, Bristol Channel.

Seint Tony—Santona, the town and port on the coast of Spain. The hill of Santona, on the northern side of the port, is a good landmark.

Seint Vincent—Cape St. Vincent, the south-west point of Portugal.

Seke up, *i.e.*, fetch, a word used nautically in the sense of to reach, or arrive at.

Seven Stonys—The Seven Stones, a cluster of rocks off the Land's End.

Seyn hede, The—The headland forming the entrance to the Seine, near Havre.

Shelde, The—Cromer, the well-known watering-place on the coast of Norfolk (*see* Introductory Remarks). "Sheld", derived from "shell", in the Suffolk dialect meant pied, of two colours, variegated ; hence sheld-apple and sheldrake, a beautifully coloured duck. It is possible that the word may have been applied to Cromer on account of the variegated colour of its sands. Cf. Moor's *Suffolk Words and Phrases.*

Shipman hede—Shipman Head, on Bryer, one of the Scilly Isles.

Siete of, By—Within sight.

Skarres and **Skarris**—Skerries harbour, east coast of Ireland, in county Meath.

Skidwhalles—Probably Stidwall Island, in Carnarvon bay, west coast of Wales.

Slade, The—The Sledway, or fairway channel into Harwich from the east.

Smal and **Smale**—Smalls rocks ; a cluster of low and very dangerous rocks off St. David's Head.

Sowdyng—Sounding.

Sowm, Watir of—The river Somme.

Spetis—Spits, banks, or sands, generally projecting from the coast. Those here referred to are probably off Shoeburyness, or Sheerness.

Spone, The—Spurn Head, the point of Holderness, at the mouth of the Humber. In 1677, according to Camden, a lighthouse was built here by one Mr. Justinian Angel, of London.

Stalmay—Scalme, now Skomer Island, south of St. Bride's Bay.

Stepilhorde—Probably Steephill near Ventnor, "horde" being merely a termination having the sense of "place", like the German "ort".

Steple—Probably the steeple of St. Peter's Church, Broadstairs, one of the marks for clearing the Goodwin Sands.

Stert, The—Start point (from the Anglo-Saxon *Steort*, a tail or promontory), a rocky headland in the south of Devonshire.

Straitis and **Straites, The**—*See* **Marrok**.

Stremes of flode—Strong tidal currents; the allusion in our text is probably to the well-known *Bore* in the Bristol Channel.

Strotarde—Struysaert, on the coast of Normandy, north of Havre.

Talamont—Talmont bank forms the eastern side of the channel leading up the Garonne.

Temesse—The Thames.

Tenet—Isle of Thanet.

Thursay—Dursey Head on Dursey island, north-west from Mizan Head.

Tilmouth—Tynemouth Haven, at the mouth of the Tyne.

To gidre and **to gidir**—Together. "Togidir", with the same meaning, occurs in Lydgate's poems.

Torre, Ilonde of—Tory Island, off the north-west coast of Ireland.

Turning wynde and **flowing wynd**—A ship is said to be "turning" or beating to windward with a head wind, a "turning wind" would, therefore, be contrary to the course to be sailed; a "flowing wind" would be abeam when a ship could sail with a flowing sheet.

Tuskarde—The Tuskar, a remarkably high rock, 20 feet above water at high tide, lying E.S.E. ¼ E. of Carnsore point, and 43 leagues N. by E. ¾ E. from the Longships lighthouse.

Updraughtis—Probably the same as "Indraughts", a term applied to the action of tidal currents in bights and bays along the coast. "Indraught" applying to the set of the flood tide, "outset" to the ebb.

Uschante—The Island of Ushant, or Ouessant, 10 miles off the N.W. coast of France, in the department of Finisterre. The shores are steep, craggy, and surrounded by rocks.

Use—Ile d'Yeu bears from the Ile du Pilier S.S.W. ¼ W., and is 19 miles distant from the Four lighthouse S. ¼ W., 37 miles, and from Belle Ile S. by E. ½ E. distant 45 miles. The island is 5 miles long and 2 miles broad, and has an extent of 77 square miles. The town of Port Breton and a fort are on its northern side.

Vaion—*See* **Baion**.

Vamborough—Bamborough Castle, on the coast of Northumberland, standing on a rocky foundation of considerable elevation.

> "Thy tower, proud Bamborough, marked they there,
>   King Ida's castle, huge and square,
>   From its tall rock look grimly down,
>   And on the swelling ocean frown."

(Marmion, Canto ii.)

Vas Glenaunt—Iles de Glenant, or the Glenan Ilands, a cluster of small islands, surrounded by rocks both above and under water, some extending 2½ miles from the main body. The navigation of these islands is beset by dangers, and the warning in our text amply justified. The Iles de Glenant, also known as the East Penmark Islands (*q. v.*), are off the coast of Finisterre.

Velafade, Toure of—The old Head of Kinsale was also known as Cape de Velho. On it stood a ruined castle with three towers, the centremost of these being a good landmark. A lighthouse, seen for a distance of 23 nautical miles at sea, now stands here. The bearings, however (north and south with Waterford), given in the text are incorrect.

Wasshe groundis, The—Watchett, on the south shore of the Bristol Channel. The approach to this place is obstructed by a shaft of rocks and beds of rolling stones.

Watir forde, Toure of—The high, white tower east of Waterford haven, since replaced by the Hook lighthouse, visible at sea for a great distance.

Waymouth—Weymouth.

Welbank—The Well, a large shoal south of the Dogger bank.

Wiet—Isle of Wight, anciently called Wiht.

Weris—The weirs or dams raised to protect Harwich harbour from the sea.

Whitevies half—Whitby Haven. The haven is almost dry at low water.

Wiklowe—Wicklow.

Winterbornes and **Wyntir. burnes**—Winterton, on the coast of Norfolk, north of Yarmouth.

Wolueshorde—On some old charts marked "Wolveshord", on others Wolfert's Head, at the southern extremity of the Isle of Wight, now St. Catherine's Point. The old name may still be traced in Woolverton, a ruined gabled manor house, said to have been built by John de Wolvert in the reign of Edward I. The *Safeguard of Sailers* (p. 41) calls the headland "Wolfer horne".

Wose and **Woyse**—Ooze or mud.

Yokelis, The—Youghal, south coast of Ireland, on old charts written Yoghill.

LONDON:
WHITING AND CO., SARDINIA STREET, LINCOLN'S INN FIELDS.

E

40°

MEDITERRANEAN SEA

35°

0°   4°

F S Weller lith.

Out

THE
HAKLUYT SOCIETY.
1889.

THE HAKLUYT SOCIETY, established for the purpose of printing rare or unpublished Voyages and Travels, aims at opening by this means an easier access to the sources of a branch of knowledge, which yields to none in importance, and is superior to most in agreeable variety. The narratives of travellers and navigators make us acquainted with the earth, its inhabitants and productions ; they exhibit the growth of intercourse among mankind, with its effects on civilisation, and, while instructing, they at the same time awaken attention, by recounting the toils and adventures of those who first explored unknown and distant regions.

The advantage of an Association of this kind consists not merely in its system of literary co-operation, but also in its economy. The acquirements, taste, and discrimination of a number of individuals, who feel an interest in the same pursuit, are thus brought to act in

THE
HAKLUYT SOCIETY.

1889.

T HE HAKLUYT SOCIETY, established for the purpose of printing rare or unpublished Voyages and Travels, aims at opening by this means an easier access to the sources of a branch of knowledge, which yields to none in importance, and is superior to most in agreeable variety. The narratives of travellers and navigators make us acquainted with the earth, its inhabitants and productions ; they exhibit the growth of intercourse among mankind, with its effects on civilisation, and, while instructing, they at the same time awaken attention, by recounting the toils and adventures of those who first explored unknown and distant regions.

The advantage of an Association of this kind consists not merely in its system of literary co-operation, but also in its economy. The acquirements, taste, and discrimination of a number of individuals, who feel an interest in the same pursuit, are thus brought to act in voluntary combination, and the ordinary charges of publication are also avoided, so that the volumes produced are distributed among the Members at little more than the cost of printing and paper. The Society expends the whole of its funds in the preparation of works for the Members; and since the cost of each copy varies inversely as the whole number of copies printed, it is obvious that the members are gainers individually by the prosperity of the Society, and the consequent vigour of its operations.

Gentlemen desirous of becoming Members of the Hakluyt Society should intimate their intention to the Secretary, MR. E. DELMAR MORGAN, 15, *Roland Gardens, S.W.*, or to the Society's Agent for the delivery of its volumes, MR. CHARLES J. CLARK, 4, *Lincoln's Inn Fields;* when their names will be recorded, and on payment of their subscription of £1 : 1 to Mr. CLARK, they will receive the volumes issued for the year.

Members and the general public are informed that the Council has approved of the following scheme for the disposal of its surplus stock.

To NEW MEMBERS.—*Complete sets of back publications*, omitting Nos. 1, 2, 3, 5, 6, 13 and 19, to be sold for . . . . £25.

To MEMBERS ONLY.—*A limited number of sets up to* 1883 inclusive, omitting Nos. 1—13, 19, 36 and 37. 53 vols. in all, to be sold for . . . . £15 15s.

To THE PUBLIC GENERALLY.—*Also, a limited number of single copies* as follows :—

Nos. 17, 22, 23, 26, 29, 31, 34, 40, 47, 50, at . . . . 8s. 6d.

Nos. 14 and 15, 21, 24, 25, 28, 30, 35, 46, 48, 51, 53, 55, 56, 58, 60 and 61, 62, 69, at 10s.

Nos. 16, 18, 20, 27, 32, 33, 38, 39, 41 to 45, 49, 52, 57, 63, at 15s.

Nos. 36 and 37, 54 and 59, at . . . . . . 20s.

₄ Subject in case of Members to a discount of 15%.

Members are requested to bear in mind that the power of the Council to make advantageous arrangements will depend in a great measure on the prompt payment of the subscriptions, which are payable in advance on the 1st of January, and are received by MR. CHARLES J. CLARK, 4, *Lincoln's Inn Fields, W.C.* Post Office Orders should be made payable to MR. CHARLES J. CLARK, at the *West Central Office, High Holborn.*

WORKS ALREADY ISSUED.

1—The Observations of Sir Richard Hawkins, Knt.,

In his Voyage into the South Sea in 1593. Reprinted from the edition of 1622, and edited by Capt. C. R. DRINKWATER BETHUNE, R.N., C.B.
(First Edition out of print. See No. 57.) Iffued for 1848.

2—Select Letters of Columbus.

With Original Documents relating to the Difcovery of the New World. Translated and Edited by R. H. MAJOR, Esq., of the Britifh Mufeum.
(First Edition out of print. See No. 43.) Iffued for 1849.

3—The Discoverie of the Empire of Guiana,

By Sir Walter Raleigh, Knt. Edited, with copious Explanatory Notes, and a Biographical Memoir, by SIR ROBERT H. SCHOMBURGK, Phil.D., etc.
(Out of print.) Iffued for 1850.

4—Sir Francis Drake his Voyage, 1595.

By Thomas Maynarde, together with the Spanifh Account of Drake's attack on Puerto Rico. Edited from the Original MSS. by W. D. COOLEY, Esq.
Iffued for 1850.

5—Narratives of Early Voyages

Undertaken for the Difcovery of a Paffage to Cathaia and India, by the Northweft, with Selections from the Records of the worfhipful Fellowfhip of the Merchants of London, trading into the Eaft Indies ; and from MSS. in the Library of the Britifh Mufeum, now firft publifhed ; by THOMAS RUNDALL, Esq.
(Out of print.) Iffued for 1851.

6—The Historie of Travaile into Virginia Britannia,

Expreffing the Cofmographie and Commodities of the Country, together with the manners and cuftoms of the people, gathered and obferved as well by thofe who went firft thither as collected by William Strachey, Gent., the firft Secretary of the Colony ; now firft Edited from the original manufcript in the Britifh Mufeum, by R. H. MAJOR, Esq., of the Britifh Mufeum.
(Out of print.) Iffued for 1851.

7—Divers Voyages touching the Discovery of America

And the Iflands adjacent, collected and publifhed by Richard Hakluyt. Prebendary of Briftol in the year 1582. Edited, with Notes and an introduction, by JOHN WINTER JONES, Esq., of the Britifh Mufeum.
Iffued for 1852.

8—A Collection of Documents on Japan.

With a Commentary by THOMAS RUNDALL, ESQ.
Iffued for 1852.

9—The Discovery and Conquest of Florida,

By Don Ferdinando de Soto. Tranflated out of Portuguefe by Richard Hakluyt ; and Edited, with notes and an introduction, by W. B. RYE, Esq., of the Britifh Mufeum.
Iffued for 1853.

10—Notes upon Russia,

Being a Tranflation from the Earlieft Account of that Country, entitled Rerum Muscoviticarum Commentarii, by the Baron Sigifmund von Herberftein, Ambaffador from the Court of Germany to the Grand Prince Vafiley Ivanovich, in the years 1517 and 1526. Two Volumes. Tranflated and Edited, with Notes and an Introduction, by R. H. MAJOR, Esq., of the Britifh Mufeum.
Vol. I. *Iffued for* 1853.

11—The Geography of Hudson's Bay.

Being the Remarks of Captain W. Coats, in many Voyages to that locality, between the years 1727 and 1751. With an Appendix, containing Extracts from the Log of Captain Middleton on his Voyage for the Difcovery of the North-west Passage, in H.M.S. "Furnace," in 1741-2. Edited by JOHN BARROW, Esq., F.R.S., F.S.A.

Iffued for 1854.

12—Notes upon Russia. Vol. 2.

Iffued for 1854.

13—Three Voyages by the North-east,

Towards Cathay and China, undertaken by the Dutch in the years 1594, 1595 and 1596, with their Difcovery of Spitzbergen, their refidence of ten months in Novaya Zemlya, and their fafe return in two open boats. By Gerrit de Veer. Edited by C. T. BEKE, Esq., Ph.D., F.S.A.
(First Edition out of print. See No. 54.) *Iffued for* 1855.

14-15—The History of the Great and Mighty Kingdom of China and the Situation Thereof.

Compiled by the Padre Juan Gonzalez de Mendoza. And now Reprinted from the Early Tranflation of R. Parke. Edited by SIR GEORGE T. STAUNTON, Bart. With an Introduction by R. H. MAJOR, Esq. 2 vols.

Iffued for 1855.

16—The World Encompassed by Sir Francis Drake.

Being his next Voyage to that to Nombre de Dios. Collated, with an unpublifhed Manufcript of Francis Fletcher, Chaplain to the Expedition. With Appendices illuftrative of the fame Voyage, and Introduction by W. S. W. VAUX, Esq., M.A. *Iffued for* 1856.

17—The History of the Tartar Conquerors who subdued China.

From the French of the Père D'Orleans, 1688. Tranflated and Edited by the EARL OF ELLESMERE. With an Introduction by R. H. MAJOR, Esq.
Iffued for 1856.

18—A Collection of Early Documents on Spitzbergen and Greenland,

Confifting of: a Tranflation from the German of F. Martin's important work on Spitzbergen, now very rare; a Tranflation from Isaac de la Peyrère's Relation de Greenland; and a rare piece entitled "God's Power and Providence fhowed in the miraculous prefervation and deliverance of eight Englifhmen left by mifchance in Greenland, anno 1630, nine months and twelve days, faithfully reported by Edward Pelham." Edited, with Notes, by ADAM WHITE, Esq., of the Britifh Mufeum.

Iffued for 1857.

19—The Voyage of Sir Henry Middleton to Bantam and the Maluco Islands.

From the rare Edition of 1606. Edited by BOLTON CORNEY, Esq.
(Out of print.) *Iffued for* 1857.

20—Russia at the Close of the Sixteenth Century.

Comprifing "The Ruffe Commonwealth" by Dr. Giles Fletcher, and Sir Jerome Horfey's Travels, now firft printed entire from his manufcript in the Britifh Mufeum. Edited by E. A. BOND, Esq., of the Britifh Mufeum.
Iffued for 1858.

21—The Travels of Girolamo Benzoni in America, in 1542-56.

Tranflated and Edited by ADMIRAL W. H. SMYTH, F.R.S., F.S.A.
Iffued for 1858.

22—India in the Fifteenth Century.

Being a Collection of Narratives of Voyages to India in the century preceding the Portuguefe difcovery of the Cape of Good Hope; from Latin, Perfian, Ruffian, and Italian Sources, now firft tranflated into Englifh. Edited, with an Introduction by R. H. MAJOR, Esq., F.S.A.

Iffued for 1859.

23—Narrative of a Voyage to the West Indies and Mexico,

In the years 1599-1602, with Maps and Illuftrations. By Samuel Champlain. Tranflated from the original and unpublifhed Manufcript, with a Biographical Notice and Notes by ALICE WILMERE.

Iffued for 1859.

24—Expeditions into the Valley of the Amazons

During the Sixteenth and Seventeenth Centuries: containing the Journey of Gonzalo Pizarro, from the Royal Commentaries of Garcilaffo Inca de la Vega ; the Voyage of Francifco de Orellana, from the General Hiftory of Herrera ; and the Voyage of Criftoval de Acuna, from an exceedingly fcarce narrative written by himfelf in 1641. Edited and Tranflated by CLEMENTS R. MARKHAM, Esq. *Iffued for* 1860.

25—Early Indications of Australia.

A Collection of Documents fhewing the Early Difcoveries of Auftralia to the time of Captain Cook. Edited by R. H. MAJOR, ESQ., of the Britifh Mufeum, F.S.A. *Iffued for* 1860.

26—The Embassy of Ruy Gonzalez de Clavijo to the Court of Timour, 1403-6.

Tranflated, for the firft time, with Notes, a Preface, and an Introductory Life of Timour Beg. By CLEMENTS R. MARKHAM, Esq.

Iffued for 1861.

27—Henry Hudson the Navigator.

The Original Documents in which his career is recorded. Collected, partly Tranflated, and Annotated, with an Introduction by GEORGE ASHER, LL.D.

Iffued for 1861.

28—The Expedition of Ursua and Aguirre,

In search of El Dorado and Omagua, A.D. 1560-61. Tranflated from the "Sexta Noticia Hiftoriale" of Fray Pedro Simon, by W. BOLLAERT, Esq. ; with an Introduction by CLEMENTS R. MARKHAM, Esq.

Iffued for 1862.

29—The Life and Acts of Don Alonzo Enriquez de Guzman.

Tranflated from a Manufcript in the National Library at Madrid, and edited, with Notes and an Introduction, by CLEMENTS R. MARKHAM, Esq.

Iffued for 1862.

30—Discoveries of the World by Galvano,

From their firft original unto the year of our Lord 1555. Reprinted, with the original Portuguefe text, and edited by VICE-ADMIRAL BETHUNE, C.B.

Iffued for 1863.

31—Marvels described by Friar Jordanus,

Of the Order of Preachers, native of Severac, and Bifhop of Columbum ; from a parchment manufcript of the Fourteenth Century, in Latin, the text of which has recently been Tranflated and Edited by COLONEL H. YULE, C.B., F.R.G.S., late of H.M. Bengal Engineers.

Iffued for 1863.

32—The Travels of Ludovico di Varthema

In Syria, Arabia, Perfia, India, etc., during the Sixteenth Century. Tranflated by J. WINTER JONES, Esq., F.S.A., and edited, with Notes and an Intro- duction, by the REV. GEORGE PERCY BADGER.

Iffued for 1864.

33—The Travels of Cieza de Leon in 1532-50

From the Gulf of Darien to the City of La Plata, contained in the firſt part of his Chronicle of Peru (Antwerp 1554). Tranſlated and edited, with Notes and an Introduction, by CLEMENTS R. MARKHAM, Esq.

Iſſued for 1864.

34 —The Narrative of Pascual de Andagoya.

Containing the earlieſt notice of Peru. Tranſlated and edited, with Notes and an Introduction, by CLEMENTS R. MARKHAM, Esq.

Iſſued for 1865.

35—The Coasts of East Africa and Malabar

In the beginning of the Sixteenth Century, by Duarte Barbofa. Tranſlated from an early Spaniſh manuſcript by the HON. HENRY STANLEY.

Iſſued for 1865.

36—Cathay and the Way Thither.

A Collection of all minor notices of China, previous to the Sixteenth Century. Tranſlated and edited by COLONEL H. YULE, C.B. Vol. 1.

Iſſued for 1866.

37—Cathay and the Way Thither. Vol. 2.

Iſſued for 1866.

38—The Three Voyages of Sir Martin Frobisher.

With a Selection from Letters now in the State Paper Office. Edited by REAR-ADMIRAL COLLINSON, C.B.

Iſſued for 1867.

39—The Philippine Islands.

Moluccas, Siam, Cambodia, Japan, and China, at the close of the 16th Century. Antonia de Morga. Translated from the Spanish, with Notes, by LORD STANLEY of Alderley.   *Iſſued for* 1868.

40— The Fifth Letter of Hernan Cortes.

To the Emperor Charles V, containing an Account of his Expedition to Honduras in 1525-26. Translated from the Spanish by Don Pascual de Gayangos.

Iſſued for 1868.

41—The Royal Commentaries of the Yncas.

By the Ynca Garcilasso de la Vega. Translated and Edited, with Notes and an Introduction, by CLEMENTS R. MARKHAM, Esq. Vol. 1.

Iſſued for 1869.

42—The Three Voyages of Vasco da Gama,

And his Viceroyalty, from the Lendas da India of Caspar Correa; accompanied by original documents. Translated and Edited by the LORD STANLEY of Alderley.   *Iſſued for* 1869.

43—Select Letters of Christopher Columbus,

With other Original Documents, relating to his Four Voyages to the New World. Tranſlated and Edited by R. H. MAJOR, F.S.A., etc. 2nd Edit.

Iſſued for 1870.

44—History of the Imâms and Seyyids of 'Omân,

By Salîl-Ibn-Razîk, from A.D. 661-1856. Tranſlated from the original Arabic, and edited, with Notes, Appendices, and an Introduction, continuing the Hiſtory down to 1870, by GEORGE PERCY BADGER, F.R.G.S.

Iſſued for 1870.

45—The Royal Commentaries of the Yncas. Vol. 2. *Iſſued for* 1871.

46—The Canarian,

Or Book of the Conqueſt and Converſion of the Canarians in the year 1402, by Meſſire Jean de Bethencourt, Kt. Compoſed by Pierre Bontier and Jean le Verrier. Tranſlated and Edited, with Notes and an Introduction, by R. H. MAJOR, F.S.A.   *Iſſued for* 1871.

47—Reports on the Discovery of Peru,

Tranflated and Edited, with Notes and an Introduction, by CLEMENTS R. MARKHAM, C.B. *Iffued for* 1872.

48—Narratives of the Rites and Laws of the Yncas;

Tranflated from the original Spanifh Manufcripts, and Edited, with Notes and an Introduction, by CLEMENTS R. MARKHAM, C.B., F.R.S. *Iffued for* 1872.

49—Travels to Tana and Persia,

By Jofafa Barbaro and Ambrogio Contarini ; Edited by LORD STANLEY of Alderley ; and Narratives of other Italian Travels in Perfia, Tranflated and Edited by CHARLES GREY, Esq. *Iffued for* 1873.

50—Voyages of the Zeni

To the Northern Seas in the Fourteenth Century. Tranflated and Edited by R. H. MAJOR, F.S.A. *Iffued for* 1873.

51—The Captivity of Hans Stade of Hesse in 1547-55

Among the Wild Tribes of Eaftern Brazil ; tranflated by ALBERT TOOTAL, Esq., and annotated by RICHARD F. BURTON. *Iffued for* 1874.

52—The First Voyage Round the World by Magellan.

Tranflated from the Accounts of Pigafetta and other contemporary writers. With Notes and an Introduction by Lord STANLEY of Alderley. *Iffued for* 1874.

53—The Commentaries of the Great Afonso Dalboquerque,

Second Viceroy of India. Tranflated from the Portuguese Edition of 1774 ; with Notes and Introduction by WALTER DE GRAY BIRCH, Esq., F.R.S.L. Vol. 1. *Iffued for* 1875.

54—Three Voyages to the North-East.

Second Edition of Gerrit de Veer's Three Voyages to the North East by Barents. Edited, with an Introduction, by Lieut. KOOLEMANS BEYNEN, of the Royal Dutch Navy. *Iffued for* 1876.

55—The Commentaries of the Great Afonso Dalboquerque. Vol. 2.

Iffued for 1875.

56—The Voyages of Sir James Lancaster.

With Abstracts of Journal of Voyages preserved in the India Office, and the Voyage of Captain John Knight to seek the N.W. Passage. Edited by CLEMENTS R. MARKHAM, C.B., F.R.S. *Iffued for* 1877.

57—Second Edition of the Observations of Sir Richard Hawkins, Kt.,

In his Voyage into the South Sea in 1593, with the Voyages of his grand-father William, his father Sir John, and his cousin William Hawkins. Edited by CLEMENTS R. MARKHAM, C.B., F.R.S. *Iffued for* 1877.

58—The Bondage and Travels of Johann Schiltberger,

From his capture at the battle of Nicopolis in 1396 to his escape and return to Europe in 1427 : translated, from the Heidelberg MS. edited in 1859 by Professor Karl Freidrich Neumann, by Commander J. BUCHAN TELFER, R.N.; with Notes by Professor B. BRUUN, and a Preface, Introduction, and Notes by the Translator and Editor. *Iffued for* 1878.

59—The Voyages and Works of John Davis the Navigator.

Edited, with an Introduction and Notes, by Captain ALBERT H. MARKHAM, R.N., F.R.G.S. *Iffued for* 1878.

The Map of the World, A.D. 1600.

Called by Shakspere " The New Map, with the Augmentation of the Indies." To Illustrate the Voyages of John Davis. *Iffued for* 1878.

60—The Natural and Moral History of the Indies.

By Father Joseph de Acosta. Reprinted from the English Translated Edition of Edward Grimston, 1604; and Edited, with Notes and an Introduction, by CLEMENTS R. MARKHAM, C.B., F.R.S. Vol. I, The Natural History.
Iſſued for 1879.

61—The Natural and Moral History of the Indies.

Vol. II, The Moral History. *Iſſued for* 1879.

Map of Peru.

To Illustrate Nos. 33, 41, 45, 60, and 61.
Iſſued for 1879.

62—The Commentaries of the Great Alfonso Dalboquerque. Vol. 3.
Iſſued for 1880.

63—The Voyages of William Baffin, 1612-1622.

Edited, with Notes and an Introduction, by CLEMENTS R. MARKHAM, C.B., F.R.S. *Iſſued for* 1880.

64—Narrative of the Portuguese Embassy to Abyssinia.

During the years 1520-1527. By Father Francisco Alvarez. Translated from the Portuguese, and Edited, with Notes and an Introduction, by Lord STANLEY of Alderley. *Iſſued for* 1881.

65—The History of the Bermudas or Somer Islands.

Attributed to Captain John Smith. Edited from a MS. in the Sloane Collection, British Museum, by General Sir J. HENRY LEFROY, R.A., K.C.M.G., C.B., F.R.S., etc. *Iſſued for* 1881.

66—Diary of Richard Cocks.

Cape-Merchant in the English Factory in Japan, 1615-1622, with Correspondence. Edited by EDWARD MAUNDE THOMPSON, Esq. Vol. I.
Issued for 1882.

67—Diary of Richard Cocks. Vol. 2.
Issued for 1882.

68 · The Second Part of the Chronicle of Peru.

By Pedro de Cieza de Leon. Translated and Edited, with Notes and an Introduction, by CLEMENTS R. MARKHAM, C.B., F.R.S.
Issued for 1883.

69—The Commentaries of the Great ·Afonso Dalboquerque· Vol. 4.
Issued for 1883.

70-71—The Voyage of John Huyghen van Linschoten to the East Indies.

From the Old English Translation of 1598. The First Book, containing his Description of the East. Edited, the First Volume by the late ARTHUR COKE BURNELL, Ph.D., C.I.E., of the Madras Civil Service; the Second Volume by Mr. P. A. TIELE, of Utrecht.
Issued for 1884.

72-73—Early Voyages and Travels to Russia and Persia.

By Anthony Jenkinson and other Englishmen, with some Account of the first Intercourse of the English with Russia and Central Asia by way of the Caspian Sea. Edited by E DELMAR MORGAN, Esq., and C. H. COOTE, Esq.
Issued for 1885.

74—The Diary of William Hedges, Esq.,

Afterwards Sir William Hedges, during his Agency in Bengal; as well as on his Voyage out and Return Overland (1681-1687). Transcribed for the Press, with Introductory Notes, etc., by R. BARLOW, Esq., and Illustrated by copious Extracts from Unpublished Records, etc., by Col. H. YULE, R.E., C.B., LL.D.
Vol. 1, The Diary. *Issued for* 1886.

75—The Diary of William Hedges, Esq. Vol. 2.

Col. Yule's Extracts from Unpublished Records, etc.
Issued for 1886.

76—The Voyage of François Pyrard to the East Indies,

The Maldives, the Moluccas and Brazil. Translated into English from the Third French Edition of 1619, and Edited, with Notes, by ALBERT GRAY, Esq., formerly of the Ceylon Civil Service, assisted by H. C. P. BELL, Esq., of the Ceylon Civil Service. Vol. 1. *Issued for* 1887.

77—The Voyage of François Pyrard to the East Indies etc. Vol. 2, Part I.
Issued for 1887.

78—The Diary of William Hedges, Esq. Vol. 3.

Col. Yule's Extracts from Unpublished Records, etc.
Issued for 1888.

79—Tractatus de Globis, et eorum usu.

A Treatise descriptive of the Globes constructed by Emery Molyneux, and Published in 1592. By Robert Hues. Edited, with Annotated Indices and an Introduction, by CLEMENTS R. MARKHAM, C.B., F.R.S. To which is appended,

Sailing Directions for the Circumnavigation of England,

And for a Voyage to the Straits of Gibraltar. From a Fifteenth Century MS. Edited by JAMES GAIRDNER, Esq. ; with a Glossary by E. DELMAR MORGAN, Esq. *Issued for* 1888.

OTHER WORKS UNDERTAKEN BY EDITORS.

A New Voyage to the East Indies by Francis Leguat. Edited by S. PASFIELD OLIVER, Captain late Royal Artillery, etc.

The Voyages of the Earl of Cumberland, from the Records prepared by order of the Countefs of Pembroke. Edited by W. DE GRAY BIRCH, Esq., F.S.A.

Rofmital's Embaffy to England, Spain, etc., in 1466. Edited by R. C. GRAVES, Esq.

A Reprint of 17th Century Books on Seamanship and Sea Matters in General, including Captain John Smith's "Seaman's Grammar", from the edition of 1692, and Sir H. Manwayring's "Seaman's Dictionary", 1644, with extracts from unpublished MSS. Edited, with Notes and an Introduction, by H. HALLIDAY SPARLING, Esq.

Histoire de la Grande Isle Madagascar, composée par le Sieur De Flacourt, 1661. Translated and edited, with copious Notes and an Introduction, by S. PASFIELD OLIVER, Captain late Royal Artillery, etc.

The Travels of Leo Africanus the Moor, from the English translation of John Pory (1600). Edited by ROBERT BROWN, Esq., M.A., Ph.D., F.L.S., etc.

The Travels of Ibn Jobair. Edited by Professor W. ROBERTSON SMITH Fellow of Christ's College, Cambridge.

Raleigh's Empire of Guiana. Second Edition (see No. 3). Edited with Notes, etc., by EVERARD F. IM THURN, Esq.

Dampier's Voyages. Edited by Lieut. DAMPIER, R.N.

The Voyages of Foxe and James to Hudson's Bay. Edited by MILLER CHRISTY, Esq.

WORKS SUGGESTED TO THE COUNCIL FOR PUBLICATION.

Inedited Letters, etc., of Sir Thomas Roe during his Embaſſy to India.

The Topographia Chriſtiana of Coſmas Indicopleuſtes.

Bernhard de Breydenbach, 1483-84, A.D. Travels in the Holy Land.

Felix Fabri, 1483. Wanderings in the Holy Land, Egypt, etc.

Voyage made by Captain Jaques Cartier in 1535 and 1536 to the Iſles of Canada, Hochlega, and Saguenay.

Ca da Moſto. Voyages along the Weſtern Coaſt of Africa in 1454 : tranſlated from the Italian text of 1507.

J. dos Santos. The Hiſtory of Eaſtern Ethiopia. 1607.

Icelandic Sagas narrating the Diſcovery of America.

La Argentina. An account of the Diſcovery of the Provinces of Rio de la Plata from 1512 to the time of Domingo Martinez de Irala; by Ruiz Diaz de Guzman.

The Eight Letters of Pietro della Valle, written from India.

The History of Ethiopia, by Manoel de Almeida.

Journal of the Jesuit Desideri in Tibet.

Travels of Friar Rubruquis.

Voyages of Willoughby and Chancellor.

Letters of Ortelius and Mercator.

The Travels of Ibn Batuta.

Tasman's Voyages.

The Travels of Teixeiro (from the Portuguese).

Voyage of Sarmiento.

Travels of the brothers Sherley in Persia.

Ulric Schmidt's Travels in the Rio de la Plata.

LAWS OF THE HAKLUYT SOCIETY.

I. The object of this Society shall be to print, for distribution among its members, rare and valuable Voyages, Travels, Naval Expeditions, and other geographical records, from an early period to the beginning of the eighteenth century.

II. The Annual Subscription shall be One Guinea, payable in advance on the 1st January.

III. Each member of the Society, having paid his Subscription, shall be entitled to a copy of every work produced by the Society, and to vote at the general meetings within the period subscribed for; and if he do not signify, before the close of the year, his wish to resign, he shall be considered as a member for the succeeding year.

IV. The management of the Society's affairs shall be vested in a Council consisting of twenty-one members, viz., a President, two Vice-Presidents, a Secretary, and seventeen ordinary members, to be elected annually; but vacancies occurring between the general meetings shall be filled up by the Council.

V. A General Meeting of the Subscribers shall be held annually. The Secretary's Report on the condition and proceedings of the Society shall be then read, and the Meeting shall proceed to elect the Council for the ensuing year.

VI. At each Annual Election, six of the old Council shall retire, of whom three shall be eligible for re-election.

VII. The Council shall meet when necessary, for the dispatch of business, three forming a quorum, including the Secretary, and the Chairman having a casting vote.

VIII. Gentlemen preparing and editing works for the Society, shall receive twenty-five copies of such works respectively, and an additional twenty-five copies if the work is also translated.

RULES FOR THE DELIVERY OF THE SOCIETY'S VOLUMES.

I. The Society's productions will be delivered without any charge, within three miles of the General Post Office.

II. They will be forwarded to any place beyond that limit, the Society paying the cost of booking, but not of carriage; nor will it be answerable in this case for any loss or damage.

III. They will be delivered by the Society's agent, MR. CHARLES J. CLARK, 4, Lincoln's Inn Fields, to persons having written authority of subscribers to receive them.

IV. They will be sent to the Society's correspondents or agents in the principal towns throughout the kingdom; and care shall be taken that the charge for carriage be as moderate as possible.

LIST OF MEMBERS

OF THE

Hakluyt Society.

(CORRECTED TO NOVEMBER 1ST, 1889.)

Aberdare, Right Hon. Lord, F.R.S., 1, Queen's-gate, S.W.; and Duffryn, Mountain Ash, Glamorganshire.
Adair, John G., Esq., Rathdaire, Monasterevan, Ireland.
Admiralty, The (2 *copies*).
'Advocates' Library, Edinburgh.
Allahabad Public Library, India (Lt.-Col. C. A. Dodd, Secretary).
All Souls College, Oxford.
American Geographical Society.
Amherst, W. Amhurst T., Esq., M.P., Didlington Hall, Brandon.
Antiquaries, the Society of.
Army and Navy Club, 36, Pall-mall.
Astor Library, New York.
Athenæum Club, Pall Mall.

Baer, Joseph & Co., Messrs., Rossmarkt, 18, Frankfort-on-Maine.
Bain, James, Esq., 1, Haymarket.
Ball, V., Esq., 28, Waterloo-road, Dublin.
Bank of England Library and Literary Association.
Barlow, R. Fred., Esq., 5, Victoria-road, Worthing, Sussex.
Barrow, J., Esq., F.R.S., F.S.A., 17, Hanover-terrace, Regent's Park.
Basan, Marquis de.
Berlin Geographical Society.
Berlin, the Royal Library of.
Berlin University, Geographical Institute of (Baron von Richthofen), 6, Schinkelplatz, Berlin, W.
Bethell, William, Esq., Rise, Hull.
Birch, W. de G., Esq., British Museum.
Birmingham Library (The).
Birmingham Central Free Library.
Bodleian Library, Oxford *(copies presented)*.
Bombay Asiatic Society.
Boston Athenæum Library, U.S.A.
Boston Public Library.
Bowdoin College, Brunswick, Maine, U.S.A.
Bremen Museum.
Brevoort, J. C., Esq., Brooklyn, New York.
Brine, Rear-Admiral Lindesay, 13, Pembroke-gardens, Kensington.
British Museum *(copies presented)*.
Brooklyn Library, Brooklyn, U.S.A.
Brooklyn Mercantile Library.
Brown, J. Allen, Esq., 7, Kent-gardens, Ealing.
Brown, J. Nicholas, Esq., Providence, R.I., U.S.A.
Brown, H. T., Esq., Roodeye House, Chester.
Brown, Robert, Esq., M.A., Ph.D., etc., Fersley, Rydal-road, Streatham, S.W.

Bunbury, Sir E. H., Bart., 35, St. James's-street, S.W.
Bureau of Navigation, Washington, U.S.A.
Burne-Jones, E., Esq., The Grange, West Kensington, W.
Burns, J. W., Esq., Kilmahew, Dumbartonshire.
Burton, Sir Richard F., K.C.M.G., H.M. Consul, Trieste.

Cambridge University Library.
Canada, The Parliament Library.
Carlton Club, Pall-mall.
Cavendish, H. F. C., Esq., 37, Eaton-place, S.W.
Ceylon Branch, Royal Asiatic Society, Colombo.
Chetham's Library, Hunt's Bank, Manchester.
Chicago Public Library.
Christiania University Library.
Cincinnati Public Library.
Clark, J. W., Esq., Scroope House, Cambridge.
Cleary, P., Esq., 200, Clarendon-street, South Melbourne, Victoria, Australia.
Cohen, Max, & Sohn, Messrs., Kaiserplatz, No. 18, Bonn, Germany.
Colonial Office (The), Downing-street, S.W.
Congress, Library of, Washington, United States.
Constable, Archibald H., Esq., The University Press, Edinburgh.
Cooper, Lieut.-Col. E. H., 42, Portman-square, W.
Coote, Walter, Esq., The Priory, Huntingdon.
Copenhagen Royal Library.
Corning, C. R., Esq., Campagne Monnet, Morillon, Geneva.
Corning, H. K., Esq., Villa Monnet, Morillon, Geneva.
Cotton, R. W., Esq., Woodleigh, Forde Park, Newton Abbot.
Crowninshield, Colonel Benjamin W., 22, Congress-street, Boston, U.S.A.

Dalton, Rev. Canon J. N.
Danish Royal Naval Library.
Davis, N. Darnell, Esq., Georgetown, Demerara, British Guiana.
Deane, Charles, Esq., 18, Sparks-street, Cambridge, Mass., U.S.A.
Derby, The Earl of, 25, St. James's-square, S.W.
Dismorr, James Stewart, Esq., Stewart House, Gravesend.
Donald, C. D., Esq., 172, St. Vincent-street, Glasgow.
Doughty, Captain Proby, R.N., care of Messrs. Hallett & Co., 7, St. Martin's-
    place.
Dresden Geographical Society.
Drummond, E. A., Esq.
Ducie, The Earl, F.R.S., 16, Portman-square, W.
Dufosse, M. E., 27, Rue Guénégaud, Paris.
Dundas, Captain Colin M., R.N., Ochtertyre, Stirling.
Dunn, John, Esq., 78, Michigan-avenue, Chicago, U.S.A.

Eames, Wilberforce, Esq., Lenox Library, 890, Fifth-avenue, New York, U.S.A.
EDINBURGH, Rear-Admiral H.R.H. the Duke of, R.N., K.G.
Edwardes, T. Dyer, Esq., 5, Hyde Park-gate, Kensington Gore, S.W.

Foljambe, Cecil G. S., Esq., M.P., 2, Carlton House Terrace, S.W.
Foreign Office (The).
Franks, Augustus W., Esq., F.R.S., F.S.A., 103, Victoria-street, S.W.

Gadsden, Capt. Frederick Ord.
Galignani, Messrs., Paris.
Georg, H., Esq., Lyons (2 copies).
George, C. W., Esq., 51, Hampton-road, Clifton, Bristol.
Gigliucci, Signor M.
Glasgow University Library.
Godman, F. Ducane, Esq., F.R.S., 10, Chandos-street, Cavendish-square, W.

Goodison, Rev. John, U.S.A.
Gore-Booth, Sir H. W., Bart., Lissadell, Sligo.
Göttingen University Library.
Grant-Duff, Sir Mountstuart Elphinstone, G.C.S.I , York House, Twickenham.
Gray, Albert, Esq., Palace Chambers, Westminster, S.W.
Grosvenor Library, Buffalo, U.S.A.
Guildhall Library, E.C.
Guillemard, F. Henry H., Esq., 1, Mill-lane, Cambridge.

Hailstone, Edward, Esq., Walton Hall, Wakefield.
Hamburg Commerz-Bibliothek.
Harvard College, Cambridge, Massachusetts.
Heawood, Edward, Esq., B.A., F.R.G.S., Caius College, Cambridge.
Hervey, Dudley F. A., Esq.
Hiersemann, Herr Karl W., 2. Königsstrasse, Leipzig.
Hippisley, A. E., Esq., care of J. D. Campbell, Esq., C.M.G., 8, Storey's-gate,
    St. James's-park, S.W.
Hooper, George. Esq.. 2, Pembroke-gardens, W.
Horner, J. F. Fortescue, Esq., Mells Park, Somersetshire.
Horrick, Mrs. Perry, Beau Manor Park, Loughborough.
Hoskins, Rear-Admiral Sir Anthony H., K.C.B., 17, Montagu-square, W.
Howard, G., Esq., Naworth Castle, Brampton, Cumberland.
Hull Subscription Library.

India Office (20 *copies*).

Johnson, General Allen B., India Office.
Jones, Joseph, Esq., Abberley Hall, Stourport.

Kelly and Co., Messrs., Shanghai.
Kensington, South, Science and Art Department.
King's Inns Library, Henrietta-street, Dublin.
Kleinseich, M., National Library, Paris.
Krämer, Messrs., Rotterdam.

Leeds Library.
Lefroy, Lieut.-General Sir J. Henry, C.B., K.C.M.G., Penquite, Par Station,
    Cornwall.
Lisbon National Library.
Liverpool Free Public Library.
Logan, Daniel, Esq., Solicitor-General, Penang, Straits Settlements.
Logan, William, Esq. (Madras Civil Service), 21, Royal-circus, Edinburgh.
London Institution, Finsbury-circus.
Loescher, Messrs. J., & Co., Via del Corso, 307, Rome.
London Library, 12. St. James's-square.
Long Island Historical Society, Brooklyn, N.Y.
Low, Malcolm, Esq., 22, Roland-gardens, South Kensington, S.W.
Luyster, A. L., Esq., 10, Silver-street, W.C.

Mackern, George, Esq., Buenos Ayres.
Macmillan, A., Esq., 16, Bedford-street, Covent Garden, W.C.
Macmillan & Bowes, Messrs., Cambridge.
Maiden, J. H., Esq., Technological Museum. Sydney, New South Wales.
Major, R. H., Esq., F.S.A., 51, Holland-road. Kensington. W.
Malcolm, W. Elphinstone, Esq., Burnfoot, Langholm, Carlisle.
Manchester Public Free Libraries.
Mantell, Walter, Esq., Wellington, New Zealand.
Markham, Clements R., Esq., C.B., F.R S., 21, Eccleston-square, S.W.

Markham, Captain Albert H., R.N., F.R.G.S.
Massachusetts Historical Society, 30, Fremont-street, Boston, Mass., U.S.A.
Massie, Admiral T. L., R.N., Chester.
Mayne, Rear-Admiral, C.B., 101, Queen's-gate, S.W.
Melbourne, Public Library of.
Mitchell Library, Ingram-street East, Glasgow.
Morgan, E. Delmar, Esq., 15, Roland-gardens, South Kensington, S.W.
Munich Royal Library.
Munro, T. R., Esq., Armenian Ghat, Strand-road, Calcutta.
Murchison, Kenneth R., Esq., 24, Aldford-street, Park-lane, W.

Netherlands, Geographical Society of the, Nijhoff, The Hague.
Newcastle-upon-Tyne Literary and Scientific Institute.
Newcastle-upon-Tyne Public Library.
New York State Library.
Nicholl, John Cole, Esq., Merthyr Mawr, Bridgend, S. Wales.
Nicholson, Sir Charles, Bart., D C.L., The Grange, Totteridge, Herts, N.
Northbrook, The Earl of, G.C.S.I., Stratton, Micheldever Station.
North, Hon. F. H., C 3, The Albany, W.
Nutt, Mr. D., 270, Strand, W.C.

Oliver, Commander T. W., R.N., Oak Hill, Barsledon, Southampton.
Ommanney, Admiral Sir Erasmus, C.B., F.R.S., 29, Connaught-square, Hyde
    Park, W.
Ontario, Education Department.
Oriental Club, Hanover-square, W.

Paine, Mrs., Cockshutt Hill, Reigate.
Paris, Société de Geographie.
Parker, Messrs., Southampton-street, Strand.
Parlane, James, Esq., Rusholme, Manchester.
Peabody Institute, Baltimore, U.S.
Peckover, Alexander, Esq., Bank House, Wisbech.
Pennsylvania, Historical Society of, Philadelphia, U.S.
Petherick, E. A., Esq., 33, Paternoster-row, E.C.
Philadelphia, Library Company of, U.S.A.
Phillimore, Charles B., Esq., F.R.G.S., Hurley Manor House, Great Marlow.
Poor, Henry W., Esq., 45, Wall-street, New York.
Portico Library, Manchester.
Powis, Earl of, 45, Berkeley-square, W.

Raffles Library, Singapore.
Ravenstein, E. G., Esq., Albion House, 91, Upper Tulse-hill, S.W.
Rawlinson, Major-General Sir H., K.C.B., 21, Charles-street, Berkeley-square.
Reed, Mrs., Hassness, Cockermouth.
Reform Club, Pall-mall.
Richards, Vice-Admiral Sir F. W., K.C.B., United Service Club, Pall-mall, S.W.
Riggs, E. F., Esq., Washington, U.S.
Robson, J. R., Esq., Aden, Cockington, Torquay.
Rockhill, W. W., Esq., care of Fidelity Trust Company, Chestnut-street,
    Philadelphia.
Royal Colonial Institute (J. S. O'Halloran, Esq., Sec.), Northumberland-avenue,
    W.C.
Royal Geographical Society, 1, Savile-row, W. *(copies presented)*.
Royal Scottish Geographical Society, Edinburgh (John Gunn, Esq., Librarian).
Royal United Service Institution, Whitehall Yard, S.W.
Rushout, The Hon. Miss, Burford House, Tenbury, Worcestershire.
Russell, Lord Arthur, 2, Audley-square, W.

San Francisco, Mercantile Library at.
Satow, Ernest, Esq., 104, The Common, Upper Clapton, E.
Shaw-Stewart, Major-General, R.E., 61, Lancaster-gate, W.
Signet Library, Edinburgh (Thos. G. Law, Esq., Librarian).
Silver, S. W., Esq., 66, Cornhill, E.C.
Sinclair, W. F., Esq., Bombay C. S.
Snell, E. W., Esq., Kidbrooke House, Blackheath, S.E.
South African Public Library.
South Australian Legislature Library.
Stanley, Lord, of Alderley, Alderley Park, Chelford, Cheshire.
St. Andrew's University.
St. Louis Mercantile Library, U.S.A. (J. N. Dyer, Esq., Librarian).
Stockholm, Royal Library of.
Strachey. Mrs. Richard, 69, Lancaster-gate, Hyde-park, W.
Stubbs, Captain Edward, R.N., 13, Greenfield-road, Liverpool.
Surrey County School, Cranleigh, per Rev. Dr. Merriman.
Sydney Free Library.

Temple, Capt. R. C., Pioneer Press. Allahabad, India.
Thomson, Sir William, F.R.S., LL.D., The University, Glasgow.
Thurston, Sir John B., K.C.M.G., Colonial Secretary, Fiji.
Toronto Public Library.
Toronto University.
Travellers' Club, 106, Pall-mall, S.W.
Trinder, H. W., Esq., 65, Cadogan-square, S.W.
Trinity College, Cambridge.
Trinity House, The Hon. Corporation of, Tower-hill, E.C.
Trotter, Coutts, Esq., Athenæum Club, S.W.
Trübner, Herr Karl.
Trübner, Messrs., Ludgate-hill, E.C.
Trübner, N., Esq. (the late), Ludgate-hill, E.C.
Turnbull, Alex. H., Esq 7, St. Helen's-place, Bishopsgate-street, E.C.
Tylor, Professor E. B., D.C.L., The Museum House, Oxford.

Union Society, Oxford.
United States Naval Academy.
United States Navy Department, Library of, Washington, D.C., U.S.A.
University of London, Burlington-gardens, W.

Vienna Imperial Library.
Volxem, M. Jean van, Hon. F.R.H.S., 1, Rue Zinner, Brussels.

Watkinson Library, Hartford, Connecticut, U.S.A.
Webb, Captain John Sydney, The Trinity House, E.C.
Webb, William Frederick, Esq., Newstead Abbey, Nottingham.
Whiteway, R. S., Esq., Bengal Civil Service, Meerut, N.W.P., India.
Wigram, R., Esq., Longcroft, Banstead, Epsom.
Wilson, Sir Charles, R.E., K.C.B., Ordnance Survey. Southampton.
Wilson, Edward S., Esq., Melton, Brough, East Yorkshire.
Wilson, Lieut.-General J., 1, Somerset-villas, Elm-grove, Salisbury.
Worcester, Massachusetts, Free Library.
Wright, R. S., Esq., 1, Paper-buildings, Temple, E.C.

Yale College, U.S.A.
Young, Sir Allen, C.B., 18, Grafton-street, W.
Yule, Colonel H., C.B., 3, Pen-y-wern-road, Earl's-court, S.W.

Zürich, Bibliothèque de la Ville.